The Magical, Fantastical World of Springhill Farm

A place where the names are all kept vital, for the protection of strangers.

By Gregga J. Johnn

Contents

Chapters and Pictures

Chapter 1   *"The spring on Springhill Farm tastes of magic and adventure."*

Chapter 2   *"Master is oh so serious. Meh is oh so seriously sleeping."*

Chapter 3   *"A diligent nap seminar with LaMa and Hobo and led by the King of Meh."*

Chapter 4   *"Master loves to sleep beneath the big, scary Jesus."*

Chapter 5   *"Treat the horses as 13 year old bullies in a school-yard and you'll be fine"*

Chapter 6   *"Wild flowers flourish beneath the Lighthouse of Love."*

Chapter 7   *"Healing drips and waves shimmer at Nulla Point in the Sutherland Shire, Australia."*

Chapter 8   *"The little den hides under a fallen tree."*

Chapter 9   *"The golden light hovers over the garage with Luna watching from above."*

Chapter 10   *"Gentle brings forth the music from within."*

Chapter 11   *"A lookout to sea crashed over by the tumultuous waves."*

Chapter 12   *"The type of car Gentle dreamed of owning someday."*

Chapter 13	"Surrounded by and basking in nature's light."	
Chapter 14	"A drunken Bumblebee feeds on a golden pear."	
Chapter 15	"Summer sleepover with the box cradle and fold out couch beds."	
Chapter 16	"Peaz tells a tale of the Wolf King."	
Chapter 17	"A Moonbeam Faery Path glitters upon the way of hope."	
Chapter 18	"Grace and mercy comes only from the secret places."	
Chapter 19	"A shallow river dreamed of in faerie tales."	
Chapter 20	"Hobo's spirit returns faithfully to LaMa and Bumbles."	
Chapter 21	"The warmth of a den holds comfort and safety."	
Chapter 22	"The Entrance to the dungeon amphitheater was secure."	
Chapter 23	"Alf was a revoltingly adorable little schnauzer."	
Chapter 24	"Take a turn around a new corner into the setting sun."	
	"Notification of Eviction"	
Chapter 25	"New growth is restored to the Brownie Nation."	
Chapter 26	"A double portion of blessing arrived."	

Favored Authors

Featured Poetry

    Counting Crows

    "My Country" by Dorothea Mackellar

    "Invictus" by William Ernest Henley

    "What does the Fox Say" song by Ylvis

    Saint Patrick's Breastplate Prayer

Featured Songs

PHOTOGRAPHY LOCATIONS

The spring on Springhill Farm tastes of magic and adventure.

Chapter 1

A pair of yellow canine eyes blinked slowly through the underbrush. He was a newcomer to Springhill farm as were the current tenants. The girls, Mercy and Gentle, were slowly moving odds and ends into the ranch home on the hilltop as LaMa, Mercy's aging mother, tottered around inside humming to her mildly distracted self.

It was early spring and the snow was fresh off the ground. Green shooters of grass and varied wild flowers were peeking out from their sleepy coffins where winter had held them dormant. Their tiny, verdant noses tickled in the wind seeking the scent of Apollo's heat signature.

The wind bustled under the wings of crows and hawks alike, particularly supporting another newcomer . . . in that form at least. In a silent fly-by across the hill top, an old-man hawk soared in new found peace and kept his eye on Mercy, his favorite.

Mercy plodded up the hill with arms bearing loads of detritus moved from one family farm to the next. The difference was this one was hers. But her family was severely lacking now and the bubbling spring of tears welled ever fresh behind her eyes. Her smile was gone. She had no idea if she'd ever find it again. Wedging the door open with an elbow and wiggling in through the frame so as to not dislodge something from her gathered load, she allowed the door to bang on her bum and barely pulled her foot in from the closing.

Home; what on earth did that mean?

She flustered about. The detritus was dumped here, unpacked there, and all the while she did not allow her mind to dwell on the knowledge that she was only there because of him. But, he was not there. It just wasn't fair.

Gentle came up from the basement asking,

"Is Father what-a-waste coming today?"

Mercy grinned wryly despite herself. Father "what-a-waste" is what the local girls called Father Christ-bearer. A gentle soul with a goodly appearance who would make any girl a happy wife, had he not chosen his priestly vocation.

"He'll be here in about an hour." Mercy offered.

"Good," said Gentle, "the cats have taken a disliking to something in the kitchen downstairs." As if on cue, a cat began wailing a low hollow yowl that echoed loudly all the way through the floor to the upstairs kitchen. "I think the house could use a good blessing."

She popped out the back door completely unconcerned that the sense behind her comments would have caused the faint hearted to quiver and the stalwart pragmatics to scoff. Gentle smiled her secret glow as the cold wind hit her full force. Mr. Northwind ran his fingers through her hair and poked at her through the layers of cloth. Fully refreshed by such attentions, Gentle took a deep breath.

The young woman surveyed the glorious sight of her precious new home. The back door of the house opened onto the bare hillside. There were three apple trees to the left of the house, a pear tree above at the peak of the hill, and some other fruit tree down past the mini-orchard. Another goodly sized tree stood guard by the roadside ditch. It was equipped with landscaping bricks around the roots to keep him sturdy. Further across the left yard was the cow field where a small heard grazed quietly in the cool sunshine. Across the road, a neighbor's great bull bellowed at them, quite unhappy that such a plethora of lovely cows and young competition should be contained out of his snorting reach.

Two dancing willows stood watch over the cow field and the yard waving at all who might care to wave back. Gentle did so. She believed they smiled to her. She believed a lot of uncommon things. She was a dreamer.

This dreamer was fully versed in the fantastic stories of great talebearers like May Gibbs, Enid Blyton, C.S. Lewis, and of course, the father of modern fantasy, J.R.R. Tolkien. She'd allowed inklings from childhood to develop into theories that what all these authors were telling her was true: if you just believe, magic will happen. But this secret ideal, shouted out at stages and movie screens in a rousing chorus of "I do, I do, I do believe in faeries," was slowly unveiling as much, much more. Here on Springhill Farm, the temperature was settling into "just right" parameters and a forecast of magic with a sprinkling of adventure was wafting through the air.

The wolf in the shadows watched all the while, keeping a close and curious eye on his target, and she was gently unaware.

Master is oh so serious: Meh is oh so seriously sleeping.

Chapter 2

"Have you seen Meh?" Mercy asked as Gentle returned from the blustering back yard. Gentle shook her head in confusion,

"No. I'll check downstairs." She trotted down the wooden steps to the basement looking through the spindled wall into the lower kitchen and beyond to the open living space. Only Master, the twin brother of Meh, blinked his unconcerned satisfaction at her from the empty carpet. Turning right into the utility room she checked the back corners by the kitty litter and then the food bowls, but no Meh. Beyond was another wooden doorway that she slid back to enter her private chambers.

"Meh-ness?" She called softly, questioning the cozy walls of her bedroom/bathroom. Bending to her knees, she checked beneath her bed. But still no light orange kitty to be seen.

"Huhmm."

Skipping back upstairs (and almost tripped by the darker orange kitty, Master, dashing up with her), she reported her lack of finding.

"No Meh-kitty down there."

Mercy bit her lip, speaking with concern,

"He's been gone since last night."

The new occupants of Springhill farm had been settling in for only a couple of weeks now and this had been just the second time the brother cats were let outside to familiarize themselves to their new surroundings. Master had instantly claimed the great red barn as his domain with the house being his private warming quarters. There was no concern of his getting lost. But Meh, usually the cuddly homebody, was nowhere to be found. No amount of calling would bring his welcome mewing to saunter around their feet again and with Mercy's too recent loss, the pain was quite unbearable.

Gentle descended to her private bedroom to, "Chamberize" as she vaguely called it. The lights were dimmed low and she set her music to her favorite Loreena McKennitt lilting sounds. Kneeling at her bedside she began her prayers and meditations.

Rising from her state of serenity, she then wandered outside to a dark path that lead through the hay fields, avoiding the tangled and wooded gully and on toward the back scruff of undergrowth at the far end of the farm. Upon entering the scratching scrublands, a twisted, hidden kingdom began opening up to her; the realm of the Coyote Conglomeration.

Gentle walked a darkened road following her own footsteps trod many a night in these unhallowed halls. The distorted black gates pushed open easily and those loitering around just stared at her, lips curled in familiar distaste. She descended past each armored Sentry as they grew in stature the further in she purposed.

In the central throne room, there was a snarl from the inked dark that breathed upon the comfortable seat of power. She didn't even let him speak, but began,

"I want my cat back."

"What makes you think I have him?" the snarl mocked her.

"Just give him back."

The dark Coyote King leaned forward, still mocking,

"Aren't you afraid to be standing here in front of me like this?"

Gentle cocked her head to the side and briefly considered, but just stated,

"Well, if I were here alone, I would be, but you and I both know I am not."

The regal Coyote hid a brief look of horror that flash across his eyes as Gentle turned her back deliberately upon his threat and sang out her song of Light. The wind whipped around the trees about her as they lifted their hands involuntarily to the shinning silver that filtered gently through shifting grey clouds.

Upon the moonbeam, Gentle alighted and softly spread out three varied sets of wings previously kept hidden in spirit. Basking in the light, the dark sentries watched aghast as she rose higher and higher, till their dark King barked at them,

"Get back to work."

His brother, Prince Don, snapped at the scattering paws that scrambled back into their daily duties of terror and mischief.

A small while later, Gentle returned to her sister in the farm kitchen,

"Meh will be back soon."

Mercy just looked nonjudgmentally a her sister and said in curious elongation,

"OK?"

Half an hour later, Mercy and Gentle's quiet evening was interrupted by Meh's frantic eyes imploring through the big back window, begging to be let in.

A diligent nap seminar with LaMa and Hobo and led by the King of Meh.

Chapter 3

Mercy drove home from a long day at work, the numbness still allowing her to continue her routine. If she could just keep busy, she might be able to keep going. Her cell phone rang and she answered without thinking. It was another caring friend. They had heard the tragic news and offered their condolences. She thanked them mechanically and answered their questions as best as she could with the information she had been able to gather.

Yes, Quess had indeed been shot. No, the officer was unaware he didn't have his hearing aids in. Yes, he had broken down and was walking, in anger, along the roadside, and yes, he was carrying his replica WWII gun so that when he turned to see who called to him from behind, the gun turned and pointed with him. It was a head shot.

She left out the most tragic of details, that he had carefully wired the gun to his arm. It wasn't a working gun, but no one would have guessed that. He had no intention of hurting anyone . . . anyone else. Not everyone would understand that a warrior still trapped in his own private 40 year war desperately needed a warriors death. The officer who turned up at the scene was just the soldier who carried his rest for him.

Mercy thanked the well-wisher again and leaned her head back, sitting in the truck on the driveway of her farm. Suddenly, the sobbing burst out and the well-spring began drowning her sorrows. Here she sat on Springhill Farm, the only land purchase she had ever made, that she would never have had the courage to do, if he had not convinced her, encouraged her and stood by her, dreaming with her of a their own place. But now, here she was and he was gone. Where the hell was the reason in that?

As the familiar numbness consoled her aching body, Mercy stepped down from the driver's seat and plodded up to the house. Gentle's dinner smells greeted her and the television flickered, babbling the day's news and informing her that LaMa was also awake, or at least she had moved from her bed to the couch.

Glancing into the living room, she saw that in fact her mother was sound asleep on the couch with Meh smiling satisfied on top of her while Bumbles, the old tabby cat and only female pet, crashed on the floor in front of the couch. Hobo, the English Sheep-dog, lay exhausted from the exertion of living in his fourteenth year, at her feet. At least her mother had much comfort.

Gentle smiled and nodded as Mercy headed to her bedroom, "Dinner will be ready in about half an hour," she encouraged.

"OK," Mercy mumbled from her already pillow stuffed face.

At dinner, they lolloped on comfy chairs, with half of the pets scattered around the living room, watching the nebulous news.

Mercy interjected her eating,

"I had another weird Quess dream last night."

"Really," Gentle feigned casual interest, but attended carefully to the words of her sister.

"Yeah, it was weird." Mercy muttered, "Had more cats in it."

"Dreams often are." Gentle continued training her eyes to the TV and her ears to her sister.

"Quess was showing me all these dead cats." Mercy recalled.

"Cats?"

"There were about 20 of them in all different places." The recollection was disturbing.

"20." Gentle repeated to confirm the details in her mind.

"It was like he was showing me all the occurrences of dead cats through his life, from when he tried to save kittens from cruel neighbors, to finding that one he buried here on the property . . . exactly three months prior to the day that he died." Mercy tried puzzling over the oddness of it all. So much seemed heavy laden with meaning, but the meanings escaped her. Gentle conceded confused as well and set in her heart to try and seek out the significance.

"Here kitteh, kitteh, kitteh . . ." LaMa was up at the door calling to Master and Meh who had been let out to 'cat' the property again before dinner.

Mercy snorted in caustic amusement,

"I caught those two in the cat blind yesterday, coming in from work. They were scoping out the game in the cow field across the road."

Gentle giggled.

Mercy continued,

"Both of them were crouched behind the brick landscaping around the tree down the front hill, peaking over the top as if saying, 'Together we can take them!'" Mercy concluded, "Stupid cats on safari."

Gentle couldn't help laughing at her sister's great telling. She offered her own observations,

"I caught them out the back stalking a rabbit that was pretty much the same size they are, massive bunny he was." She continued, "Master was right up stalking him and Meh was back behind the fence playing back up. Of course, their quarry got away, but I wouldn't be too surprised if they figure out how to take one down soon."

"Meh hasn't come in yet." LaMa nattered, tottering back to her couch seat as Master raced from the front door, off to the food bowl. Hobo tried getting up from his floor bed but his back legs disagreed so he just allowed LaMa to pet his head and continued loyally by her feet. Bumbles pawed at LaMa's food plate, stealing scraps.

"Bumbles!" Gentle scolded and put her plate down to grab the old cat off LaMa's lap. She lifted the kitty to her face and asked, "Have you forgotten your one manner again?"

"Darn cat," Mercy grumbled.

Gentle explained, "This one is so tiny, she only has room for one manner at a time. I've only asked her to keep three, but I think she forgot the first one already."

Taking Bumbles kitty toward the door, she instructed,

"No begging, no getting on the table, and no pooping in my apartment." She carefully tossed the bag of old bones onto the warm front porch.

Bumbles sprawled in a pool of setting sun as Gentle called to Meh again,

"Kiitty, kitty, kitty, kitty, kitteeeee," still no sign of the cuddly one.

She returned to her dinner shaking her head to Mercy, who sighed,

"Of all the stupid pets to go missing, it has to be him, every time." She whispered, "He was Quess' favorite."

"I know," said Gentle, "excuse me for a minute, I need to go Chamberize."

Mercy watched her sister leave for her bedroom below in amused curiosity. She had no idea what to make of the oddness, but had seen too much randomness in the world to argue or condemn it. Instead she turned her head to the big, scary, wooden carving of Jesus on the cross that Quess had brought back from Germany (with its own airplane seat). The massive and rather gruesome crucifix held reign over the living room from the wall by the grandfather clock. The girls affectionately referred to it as burglar proofing, as few could enter their home without being accosted by the shock of the wooden depiction.

Mercy prayed,

"If you can bring him back, we'd really appreciate it."

She sighed, warmed by the simple fact that such an odd piece of art could grow on someone enough to breed affection. She did love that crucifix in all its gruesome glory. It was a comfort to have such memories about her and she had such little comfort left inside.

Master loves to sleep beneath the big, scary Jesus.

Chapter 4

Gentle took her walk across the open hay fields again, with determined purpose. The back woods loomed dark and menacing, but as their shadow stretched out toward her she leaned in toward them and stretched out her own menacing presence: her wings. As one, each of the three pairs billowed out from behind her.

On top, by the base of her neck, was the pair that looked most like a butterfly's. Thick black outlines in stark contrast to brilliant rainbows of color, block by block of shimmering rainbow light glowed and illuminated the path about her feet. These were her wings of Love.

In the center, mid-shoulder, was a pair of pure white eagle wings that had the potential to be blinding when fully unfurled. These were her wings of Faithfulness.

The lowest pair, where her ribcage met with her spine, was a pair of dragon wings for speed equipped with claws and scales of red and purple. These, the most lethal of the three, were her wings of Freedom.

It was in this state of beauty and terror that she approached the closed black gates of the Coyote Kingdom. She barely even touched them but simply brushed them open and aside. Those canine sentries near-by cowered in the shadows and she stalked straight to the central hallway. Storming down the open glade of darkness she called to the inked throne,

"What did I tell you about my cat?"

The Coyote King just looked bored at her approach, completely expectant and unrepentant, he gestured to the side,

"But he looks so good where I have him?"

Gentle turned to see her wretched kitty, eyes wide and terrified, with a vicious spiked collar around his neck that was chained in several places to a black ornamental wrought iron stand. He was a slash of pale orange in the darkness, a sarcastic nightlight for the midnight hour.

Gentle felt her anger fuming and she breathed deeply for control, unfurling her wings as they beat upon the hot air like furnace bellows.

"Yes, yes," continued the King, unconcerned, "Light, love, faithful, freedom, I know, blah, blah, blah, blah, blaahhhh." He smirked his mocking at her. Prince Don giggled in the shadows behind him. "I just can't resist taking him and poking at you like this. I mean, really, you're far more entertaining than any TV show. Just look at you!"

From the edges of the hall, mirrors closed in around her on every side, and the shimmering, blinding of her own wings affected her eyes as much as anyone else's. She barely had time to flick her dragon flight and soar above the cage of mirrors that sealed itself beneath her with the slam and crack of shattering glass. From mid-air, she called to Meh, using his real name and he jumped to her, his chains dissolving in the faith that his mistress would save him.

But as she turned to leave, the King's parting taunt turned her lonely heart to fear-filled ice.

He whispered loud and clearly,

"How is your Beloved spy doing these days?"

Gentle tossed Meh beyond onto a patch of nearby clouds pushing it to safety with the wind of her wings as she flew furiously at the King. She grabbed his throat in her clutches and squeezed hissing like a ferocious siren,

"He is none of your business. You will NOT touch him." Then she retreated, quickly; glaring with all the anger and tumultuous passion a scorned woman can muster and parted there for home.

The King rubbed his scorched throat and slowly smiled a satisfied grin.

Gentle ascended back up to the living room from her Chambers and met with Mercy who was washing dishes. She just looked at her sister and said,

"Let me tell you a story."

Mercy raised her eyebrows and said,

"OK?"

"I think our cat is being . . . borrowed," was all Gentle could bring herself to say at first.

Mercy dried off her hands and prepared to hear a tale of incredulous wonder she knew was likely just too real to be made up.

Gentle regaled the events with little embellishment and played down most of the elements and generally ended with,

"Meh should be back again soon, I think."

"We'll see?" was all Mercy could acknowledge, yet still, never with even a hint of judgment.

Another half hour passed in front of the flickering comedies and soft glow of smart phones as each girl lost herself in her own social network, relaxing, giggling or laughing out loud, and sharing various pictures, until the soft, startling mew echoed in from the back window and Meh looked in with wide terrified eyes, begging entrance once again.

Gentle ran to the back door to fetch him in. Mercy walked to her bedroom muttering amused, but determined,

"I'm getting the holy water." She returned with a full mason jar.

Snuggling the big fury kitty clinging to her for warmth, Gentle questioned,

"What's that?"

"Holy water, it can't hurt?" Mercy shrugged, "Father left it here after blessing the house. He said this was the good stuff." She unscrewed the lid, "He used the script and blessings from before they were watered down, no pun intended."

She dipped her fingertips into the water and brushed Meh's head. But, Meh was having none of that and scrambled out of Gentle's arms, running off, tail flicking, and entirely just too peeved for words. He'd had enough torment for one night. Mercy flicked the last few drops after his disappearing tail and the girls laughed amused at the poor darling's disgust.

"Stupid cat," Mercy was pleased to see the tormented feline. She was so relieved to have him home she touched the base of the gruesome crucifix and whispered a thank you prayer as she walked off to bed.

Gentle woke LaMa softly and gave her the last of the day's pills with her root beer, or "awbeer" as LaMa like to call it,

"Ahhh, there's my girl, my favorite pill pusher." She giggled in her aged delight.

"Well that's just what I do for you, hon, pills and beer." Gentle winked, opened a bag of yogurt covered pretzels and set them next to a tangerine on the coffee table.

LaMa snuggled under her blanket, TV remote in hand and Bumbles sitting on her chest. Gentle cleared her throat and rubbed it a little, saying good night.

LaMa waved her off and warned,

"Keep warm, and don't catch a throat cold."

"I'll do my best, LaMa. Everyone is in now. Meh came home so we're all accounted for."

"Ooooh! That silly kitty, well I'm glad we're all in for the night." In two minutes, she would snore again before the soft TV lights.

Gentle descended to her room with a cough and a final prayer on her knees by her bed,

"Elohim: Father of Lights, Savior of Love, and Comforter of my soul, grant Beloved safe passage this evening. Keep watch over his path and grant him dignity in the decisions he makes that affect the lives of millions unaware of all he does . . . and if it be that he should tire of saving the world, send him home to me, Amen."

From outside her window a long, resounding howl echoed up into the heavens and Gentle's tears found comfort in the misery of that lonely cry.

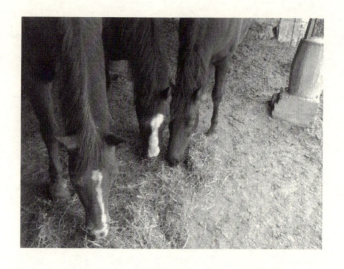

Treat the horses as 13 year old bullies in a school-yard and you'll be fine.

Chapter 5

Gentle and Mercy sat bleary eyed sipping coffee and slurping breakfast cereal soaking up the sunshine that blanketed through the window and settled on the dining table. It was Saturday morning and Mercy had set her mind to the task before her.

"I think that this morning, before I get any mowing done, I may need to mow, then when I get all that mowing done, I'm going to have to mow."

"Sounds like a plan" smirked Gentle, stretching and clearing her throat. She moved to the back door, "I need to get to the dingbats before there's a riot in the coral."

"Did you not get the memo?" Mercy jested, "They ordered breakfast fifteen minutes ago. There's going to be starvation and slaughter, if you don't get there soon."

Gentle giggled. Her customary banter with Mercy was beginning to lighten in mood. She still missed hearing her sister laugh, but knew that would come again, in time. The old hawk flew by silently and Gentle called to Mercy to look out the back window to see him.

Pulling the back door shut behind her, she followed the winged flight with shaded eyes and flitted herself down to the barn. The horses were indeed kicking on the fencing and a good scolding was snorted at her. Gentle grinned,

"Dingbats."

Macro, the lead gelding, huffed and started at Shyner, as equally big a gelding, but too unbothered to actually take any leadership. Shyner usually hung out as the bottom rung on the little herd totem, while the oldest of the horses, Codger, retired easily to Macro, the newest member of the family. Zoe, the resident brood mare and brown coat, cast herself alongside whoever was in power and then pushed her way in to claim whatever food was available, because really it was all about her and her only, as was her opinion.

"Oi," Gentle pushed into Macro, "quit being a bully to Shyner. I'm the boss when I'm here." She leaned against Macro's big head as he snuggled into her, "and don't you forget it." He nuzzled at her and Zoe pushed her nose at Gentle's hands.

"No, Madam foodie, I don't have anything in my hands for you to eat." The mare licked the salt off Gentles palm as if to say, "I beg to differ." The young woman waved her hands at the equestrian crush and scooted everyone out of her way. "Back off, so I can get to the ladder you goobers."

Gentle was not a farm girl by birth, in fact, she wasn't even really Mercy's sister. Mercy and LaMa had taken her in after she'd returned from a distant place. Gentle fit easily into the country life though, living a dream for which she'd always longed but had somehow come short of in her past. Choices being hers or imposed upon her by illness, or other's expectations, as Life often randomly throws about, those choices had taken her on many a dark trail. But, now she was tossing hay down to horses after receiving the only word of advice on horsemanship that Mercy had to offer,

"Treat them all as thirteen year old bullies in a school-yard and you'll be fine."

So, she did, and she was.

Mercy was already trundling about on the tractor mower over the hills and dales of the farm yard. She turned off the engine on the other side of the fence and called,

"We can probably let them out onto the hilltop paddock for the day. The grass has grown in enough by now."

Gentle looked at the electric fence and quickly estimated the best way of opening it up without getting trampled. She casually pranced through the poo toward the fencing and quickly had a snort-full following. She warned sternly,

"You will back off and take your time. No rushing me." She unhooked the electrified rope, keeping it tight, "You hear me?!" She walked quickly to the opposite fence post as the breaking of hooves kicked up mud and Shyner took off, with Macro close on his heels both eager to get ahead, because surely there wasn't nearly enough pasture for both of them on the entire hill top. Gentle sighed, spitting mud off her lips. "Dingbats."

Her phone barked and she smiled. Of late, there had been a few younger guys and gals messaging her for advice on love and life in general. There were two young gentlemen in particular she was aiding in their quests for love. Unfortunately, she didn't understand why their efforts were not being appreciated so she felt like she wasn't being much assistance, but was deeply grateful for the constant conversation in her particular loneliness. This barking of her phone was a younger gentleman she'd not yet met in person, but had been casually communicating with for a couple years, playing games online and being a part of the same forum of fans sharing a deep passion for things Divine and Geek.

She read the message and giggled to herself. They had taken to sending each other random cat and dog pictures as he liked to associate himself with the canine and she with the feline. Re-pocketing her phone, she wondered to herself why he kept messaging, but was so glad he did. She recalled the last time she'd been out at a party gathering with her friends and someone had suggested she and the other younger gentleman she was counseling might have romance in common. His immediate response amused her more than stung,

"Oh, shoot no. She's like my mother."

Gentle had just giggled and hugged her friend, reminding herself, she was not chronologically as young as she still felt. It was as if, those many years ago, when she determined to set aside her personal dreams and career goals to be a wife and mother that she had somehow stopped in a stasis. Deep inside, she was still twenty-three despite having been a single mother for thirteen years, single mother that is with her oldest child being only months younger than her and called husband. After her divorce and personal hiatus into hell, she had resurfaced, gone home to heal and then returned, taken in by long lost friends and was now finally living on her own terms.

Master mewed at her loudly. She called to him and they took a walk up the field hills. The wind blew away her cares and her funny little orange companion kept up as a dog might. At the top of the hill, she stretched her arms and sang a song of summer. Clear, crystal and ringing in the sounds of the glorious season. She cared not a hoot if the neighboring farms heard.

Wild flowers flourish beneath the Lighthouse of Love.

Chapter 6

Gentle squinted at the painful brilliance of her phone screen to make out the time, 3:48am. Her throat caught her breath and she coughed. Swallowing brought a searing pain and grimacing she felt the swelling around her vocal chords. The coughing began again and continued with such vengeance that she had to drag herself across the room and allow the dry heaves that suddenly wracked her body to pour something unseen into the bowl for refuse. Again, she hacked, and again, she heaved. She hoped it didn't wake Mercy sleeping in the room above.

When the convulsions subsided she crawled back across the tiled, then carpeted floor and knelt by her bed, flopped over in exhaustion. Her sweat slimed face mashed into the covers and she breathed as one spent. Her prayers sought for discernment as such episodes of physical illness were not unfamiliar to her and she knew there was a deeper understanding to be seen in the shallow physical symptoms.

Given such encouragement, she used what strength her arms had left to drag herself up and under the covers. Curling up tight and pressing herself down into the fluff of her feather tick. She pulled the feather pillows to her tummy and back, and lifted the feather comforter over her ears.

She was so grateful for the warm comforts of Mercy and LaMa's generosity. She had nothing of her own, save a top of the line smart phone that functioned as her personal business office, post office and connecting place for family, friends and acquaintances all over the world. She also had a laptop that had been bought with pay-out money from an insurance deal with a modeling company whose lights on set had accidentally been too hot and caused such a burning of her eyes that she was blinded for three days . . . a small price to pay for her business start-up necessities.

The only other possession in her name was her car that Mercy had covered half of the selling price with bartered hay to feed Macro. These were her only real physical possessions (apart from clothing and expendables).

Ohhh, but she was rich with wealth beyond abundance. She smiled, holding tight to thoughts of her reason for returning out of her healing walkabout: her three sons. Giggling to herself, she acknowledged the mama pride as she knew without a shadow of a doubt that her boys were indeed the coolest darn folk she'd ever had the privilege to know. It was just the best blessing of all that those awesome dudes, happened to have been born of her.

Gentle's eyes welled up with tears of deep gratitude for all that her life held. Then heeding the call, she closed her eyelids and descended into her memory palace.

It wasn't really a palace. She'd heard about it from Mercy whose reading came across the idea used as a tool by spies and other such busy people needing to keep too many secrets to access at once. Gentle loved the idea because her past illness had stripped her of many precious memories, most of them being of her sons during their early years. But she just knew that those images were still with her, somewhere, she just had to find them.

Meditation and relaxation had also become a habitual tool to combat the past anxiety and stress that had once crippled her soul. So she decided to combine both ideas and in quiet moments as these, in the dark before the dawn, she slowly and deliberately began fashioning in her mind a "memory palace." With her imagination and storytelling default, however, the palace idea quickly expanded into a multi leveled, multi-dimensional, Island floating in the black of her subconscious.

Gentle stood on her island. Her place of peace and restoration, full of places yet to explore and wonders yet to discover and rediscover as she was sure her past memories were all kept here. She must be careful where she looked though as some memories are better left undisturbed in the dark, until the timing is right.

She never really explored the island. In fact, most days she spent either in the Light house cuddling on the Lap of Love, or standing on the peninsular looking out to sea, hoping for a worthy Captain to come to love her. It was rather pathetic she admitted, but didn't care. This was her place to be all she was; good, bad and anything else. Here she was free to be.

She cleared her throat, climbing the circular stone steps of the Lighthouse. She sensed His closeness and skipped up the last passage, running into the blessed Presence. Snuggling deep into the restoration of unconditional Love she heard the Voice of discernment,

"Remember when you strike out in anger, you give away your protection."

Gentle cleared her throat and humbled her natural arrogance, pride and self-justification.

"I remember. Forgive my temper attack on him." She recalled her strangling efforts to silence the Coyote King.

"Already done," a scarred hand caressed her hair tenderly.

"What are the consequences?" Gentle asked, wondering if the coughing and heaving had healed the issue.

The Voice smiled and pointed to a tiny cage where an even tinier imp cowered. It hissed at her,

"I hass your voissse." He held his tiny hands clutched to his black and wrinkled chest.

Gentle checked to make sure Immanuel's presence was still guiding her, then stepped down to the cage and opened it holding out her hand,

"I need that back. Give it, please."

The imp grumbled but complied and dropped a small, crumpled, and damaged package into her hand. Gentle sighed,

"Go on." She nodded down toward the steps. It looked gleefully at the freedom offered then skeptically snapped, "you gonna to doos harm on my backs?" He slunk into the far end of the cage away from the open door.

"No," said Gentle, "You're free to go and hide from your master wherever you can until he finds you."

The imp's eyes widened in horror, then he skittered out of the cage, but instead of rushing down the steps he found a mouse hole and disappeared.

Gentle brought the bruised and battered package to the seat of Love and gave it over.

"All that I have, just as it is, is Yours to do with as You will."

Immanuel smiled and whispered into her ear,

"And I will do such wonders with you that the entire world will stand in awe."

"Make me . . ." she faltered,

"What is your desire, dear heart?" He asked genuinely hoping to hear her speak it.

With fear, blinded by faith, Gentle prayed,

"Make me a Niagara waterfall of your Love that all who come near will be wet with the rain of Your presence, be it mist, or full drenching, pending how close they choose to be drawn to You." This was her familiar prayer that had been her heart's cry for some time now, but then she took a deep breath and added a new request, "and make me Your billboard to show off Your glory and the wonder of what You can do with a fully surrendered heart." She opened her tear filled eyes of hope and saw that He, too, smiled with tears in His eyes. She loved Him so much, "Show off in my life, LORD, show off just what You can do. Amen."

"So be it, and AMEN." The Voice of Elohim echoed deep in Love.

Healing drips and waves shimmer at Nulla Point in the Sutherland Shire, Australia.

Chapter 7

The early spring air was still cool in the morning and Gentle drew her cardigan close around her bruised and swollen neck. Her voice was completely gone to the throat cold she'd contracted and she cleared the excess mucus painfully from her vocal chords and swallowed with a grimace. But, the rising sun shone directly upon her as she stood in the back door and she embraced the gentle heat with as deep a breath as her throat would allow.

The fields were flowering and beckoning her to explore so, with phone in hand; Gentle secured her ear-buds and turned up her favorite playlist of random songs. Smiling in the natural atmosphere, she ducked through the barbed wire fence out into the paddock with the horses.

Codger was the first to greet her and Zoe pushed in quickly, as well, just in case there was food to be had. Macro wandered toward them while Shyner stood aloft, unbothered by the fuss. Gentle greeted and nuzzled with each one, even walking to Shyner to admire his red coat in the sunshine. Meh-kitty picked through the growing grass, mewing loudly, not wanting to be left behind.

Sitting on a patch of green on the top of the paddock hill, Gentle closed her eyes. Surrounded by the animals, she felt so close to the natural world and reached out her own atmosphere to be one with all the energies of the air, light, and even electricity that flowed through the unseen world about her. Laying down she rustled her fingers through the dirt and grass. Meh nuzzled her for an ear scratching and Zoe snuffled at the grass, grazing by her head. The spring of water bubbled quietly at the base of the hill, always maintaining 51 degrees year round, and the music echoed in her ears through modern technology and metal. All this ignited the fire in her soul and it burned loudly.

Gentle clamped her eyes shut as that bane of her weakness rose up and randomly kicked in. Her back arched with the wracking muscle spasms that filled her body full of tension and pleasure. Yet tears of distress slid down her cheeks for there was no controlling it. The burning within was the last of her illness that lingered and continued to torment.

Too many nights, she had succumbed to the passion of desire in dark places. Too many "helpful gentlemen" had assisted her in draining her passions both as friends and strangers. This was the paradox of her love. Gentle sought only to be a beacon of light, hope, acceptance and compassion, but the flip side, the dark yin to her light yang was an unrelenting temptation that sought to devour her heart and the heart of any man that came near.

There was more to Gentle than just three pairs of unseen spirit wings. There were three whole-parts that came with them. The one that tormented now was the Siren.

Once she had been separated, shattered and un-sanity had controlled her mind, but during her walkabout there had come much healing. Gentle had spent two years meditating, journaling, and being comforted marvelous much by family and the ocean. The water was her great healing place, specifically the beaches of Cronulla and the Southerland Shire in Australia. So, now, in her return to claim what was left behind, her once separated disassociations had been re-absorbed, re-aligned, and re-assimilated into a multi-faceted personality.

The black coal of her burned out life had once been crushed and broken. It was this charcoal dust and crumbled soul she had surrendered to Elohim, just as she had surrendered her bruised and damaged voice box that the Imp had stolen.

Elohim had taken her life, from even before she thought to give it, He had pressurized and held tight the crushing dark that assaulted her. He pressed in on all sides. He took the raw mess, and carved with His Words of Life; the unbreakable, laser-light of clear Love, and He had cut and cut and cut away what was not necessary. He polished and pressed, and washed and cleaned, shined and brought forth a diamond with many facets.

Gentle looked at her life, gleaming and shimmering still in the dark, hidden away and waiting. She had multiple views on how the world looked. Some of these views were even yet unknown to her. The strongest and closest were those of her freedom and her love. Elohim had cast in her His own faithfulness and had given her also Love and Freedom born of black coal, pressed in and made shining new.

Of course, there was still much to be done. Here on the hilltop tormented by agonizing random attacks of lingering chemicals and hormones out of balance, Gentle surrendered again to the process of healing. She breathed deep and let what was wash over her. She cried, many nights and days in loneliness and confusion. Why had all those she loved not wanted to make the effort to love her in return? Yes, she was incredibly difficult to love and had a passion and wild soul that only the strongest could ever hope to manage. Was there a man strong enough?

She thought she'd met such a one. He was very strong. In fact, he carried the weight of the world upon his shoulders so deftly that no one would take responsibility for the decisions he made but himself alone. Those decisions were based upon years of military and business administration experience. He was a sought after man. But, he had confessed personally and privately to her that he would give up all the travel and glamor and secret danger if only he could have the simplicity of love and family. She'd mocked him in that moment. She told him,

"No you wouldn't. I'm right here and you are not choosing me."

He only sighed and concurred with his inability to have a relationship with any one whether he loved them or not; he chose his career. He chose to continue to fight to save the world. In that was his nobility defined and glorified.

Yet, Gentle, was left alone.

Her phone barked again, and she smiled though the tears, but with gratefulness this time. Another kitty and puppy picture soothed her with a laugh. Then up from the gully came a small howl, quiet and consoling. Gentle wondered who the wolf was and wandered back to the house to make dinner.

The little den hides under a fallen tree.

Chapter 8

Sitting on the telephone pole, feathers unruffled by the wind, the old man hawk twitched his head side to side, watching the quiet house in the morning hours. The weather was warming quickly and the sun already streaked across the dawn as his feathers stiffened, stilling even his own heart beat so he could hear her. She stirred within.

Mercy rolled in her bed waking slowly, sadly, as the tears washed her pillow. She whispered his name. There was no whisper back. Her job called to her instead so she made her way quietly around the house and headed out to the days duties.

The hawk, outside, stretched his wings and flew off, heavy on the wind, and south to his duty.

Gentle rose up out of her morning meditations at an hour that most who worked a full time job would consider luxuriously late. Gentle however, stretched and felt fully content having already completed a good half-day's work in her imaginings. That evening she would have to go to her part time job, so there was much more to be done making sure LaMa was fed and pilled, the house relatively ordered with dishes clean for use, a little dinner to share when Mercy came home, the next writing project chipped away at, and, oh, yeah . . .

"Mreoooow," Bumbles complained at her feet,

The pets all needed to be fed.

Gentle pulled on some jeans and supportive wear and climbed the wooden basement steps. She sneaked into LaMa's bedroom and helped ancient Hobo up on his arthritic legs and out to the door so as to avoid having to scrub the carpet again. Master and Meh decided to join the morning walk and dashed into the sunshine. Gentle closed the front door and left via the back mud porch picking up a little wicker basket. Stepping down onto the back step she was immediately greeted by obsessive moos to her left.

"Yes, yes, good morning boys," Gentle giggled, waving to the cluster of steers accosting her appearance with demands for treats.

Even the horses trotted up to the barbed fencing over-looking the back yard snorting at her as the smell of early summer apples was heavy on the wind. Gentle floated over to the three apple trees and greeted them by name,

"Good morning, Stella and Stanwick, have you a plethora of bounty for me today? What of you Stodgington? Have you begun dropping yet?" She ran her fingers through the leaves of the heavy laden trees and knelt down to clear the grass beneath.

Mercy found a continuous need to mow the very fertile grass that loved to reach skywards excessively in the effervescent after effects of rain. But, trying to mow was difficult around apple trees that covered the ground beneath with masses of rotting fruit, so Gentle spent an hour every day picking up the discarded flesh and sharing it with the farm herds, much to their delight. The cows mooed impatiently and the horses snorted at her. It was like natures sweet cadence of,

"Where are my apples, dammit?"

The first basket full was dumped at the cows' feet. They still were not quite accustomed to human interaction so the stinky boogers backed up and then stampeded the mess when Gentle stepped away. The countrified gal laughed at them noticing how adorably disgusting cows really were and crooned at their snot filled snuffling,

"Enjoy, you big goobers. You're going to taste so yummy come fattened season." She laughed at her own callousness.

A second and a third basket was tossed over to them while the horses stamped rudely at the hilltop fence. Gentle stood quietly, talking softly. The steers had names that were more the numbers on their ear tags.

"Hey mister 19, you are getting big aren't you." She reached with slow motion toward the apple snuffling head. 19 was the biggest of the four, the oldest, and the least cowardly. He allowed her to scratch his forehead because he was too busy eating as many apples as he could stuff into his face before the other cows got to them. Numbers 18 and 13 shied away from her still, and "no-tag" sneezed his sloppy drool behind them all.

"Eww," Gentle screwed up her nose in delight at the docile creatures and returned to pick up the last of the apples for the horses.

Zoe and Shyner were pushing on the barbed wire fence, in fact, as Gentle walked closer up the hill she saw Shyner's whole front chest scratched up with bare patches from the barbed wire,

"Really," Gentle questioned in frustration at the idiocy of the need to feed? She dumped the apple basket at their feet before Zoe could tip it out of her hands and rubbed Shyner's chest making sure the skin wasn't bleeding, "Dingbats."

Codger and Macro quickly joined the group as Gentle returned to kneel beneath the apple trees fetching the last few not quite so rotting apples off the grass. A bee or two buzzed around the sweet scents and the woman sat back on her feet, breathed deep the warmth of the sun, and waved her body in the soft breeze. Crows called in the distance and one landed on a post across the road from her. She frowned and searched for a second.

"Where's your buddy, Mr. Crow? I don't want you here on your own." Gentle recalled the children's rhyme Counting Crows, "I will have no sorrow today."

The bull across the road bellowed at her and she stood to throw, with all her strength, a single apple to him, casually scaring off the "one is for sorrow" feathers.

The black omen fluffed up into the air and soared over to a nearby tree sitting a couple of branches below another big black crow. Gentle smiled a satisfied grin and crooned at them,

"Two is for mirth, that's much better."

The last basket of apples was deposited at the hooves of the horse herd and Gentle took off on a morning safari to the ravine behind their paddock.

The ravine was a mess and tangle of untamed trees, both fallen and new growth. It was quiet and she took a few pictures with her phone of the lovely circle of Life, dying and living, breathing and continuing around her. She found a nestling spot under a fallen tree that had a den-like appearance to it and thought briefly of the wolf, but this den was far too small for such a creature.

On her way back to the house to continue with the rest of the days doting's Gentle heard a rustle and slowly crouched, turning to glance behind. A small red fox darted under the bushes in the direction from which she had just come. Gentle smiled and whispered to herself,

"Hallo Mister Fox, what do you have to say to the world today?" giggling in her own amusement Gentle continued down the hill humming a familiar viral tune to herself.

The golden light hovers over the garage with Luna watching from above.

Chapter 9

Fumbling with the padlock on her locker, Gentle finally pulled the metal door open, tossed her name badge inside, and prepared to leave work for the night. She used to care about her job. She used to take great pride in running her little corner of the store with speed, efficiency and order until she realized that her months of effort all came to naught when those superior in status came by and made changes with what seemed to be a bigger perspective, but just ended up making a bigger mess.

At first she was infuriated by having her hands tied so ridiculously that it made her job impossible to keep either herself or her co-workers truly safe from injury. Her pleas for change fell on deaf ears, so in the end she succumbed to the only conclusion that everyone else worked under; just stop caring.

She sighed and discarded the natural frustration in weariness and determined to burn off the pent up energy the best way she knew how. It was karaoke night at her local, "Murmurs" pub.

The parking lot was dark and the moon shone full tonight with the freedom from another evening spent grinding for someone else. Each new clarifying breath carried her closer to the car. Her phone barked and she grinned.

She still had no clue why he kept messaging,

"How was work tonight?" he inquired.

The only male in the entire universe who ever bothered to notice what her work schedule was and it had to be him.

She responded with a nebulous,

"Same crap, not enough shovels" that pushed him back into that void socially known as the friend zone. She couldn't even look at him, but after a quick, "I'm driving now," to dismiss him again, she buried her phone in her pocket after seeing his,

"Of course you are," flash across the screen.

She picked up speed down the highway hoping her forbidden fruit might be about tonight.

Her heartbeat picked up more as she rounded the corner of the dark streets and saw all the chrome glistening in the parking lot.

The Siren within grinned in glee,

"The boys were here tonight."

Gentles teeth snapped at the air as she walked from her car and an inner growling gurgled in her throat. Straightening her back, tossing her hair aside she smiled openly at the rough gentlemen that smoked near the door. Someone played cavalier and she thanked them directly and sauntered through the door held open.

Inside, the music was loud, the beer was flowing and the spirits lifted up all lonely hearts, if but for a couple of hours. She glanced to the stage where her dear bar-buddy gal was already singing. Mid song, that gal waved and pointed to the bar over the microphone. Gentle knew what she was pointing at, before she even looked,

"Yes, he was there tonight."

As she sat quietly next to him, his face buried in the luminous amusements of a smart phone, a neighboring mate called to her,

"How are you doing tonight, sweetheart?"

Gentle leaned over the one next to her and called to the other in a loud telling Australian accent,

"I'm bloody marvelous, thank you."

The soldier next to her grinned without even looking up.

She ordered her usual soda and he dropped his phone on the bar,

"Is that all you're drinking tonight?" he teased.

She winked at him,

"That's what I'm starting with." What she didn't say was that was all she could afford and she was stretching her budget just to get that instead of the typical water.

"Hey, sexy mama!" Little Mandy hugged her from behind, "I put your name down to sing tonight."

Gentle jumped off her stool to squeeze her bud. Other friends were there, too, and she made the rounds greeting everyone, including some of the dear, rough, gentlemen riders.

One such independent rider, and kindred soul, was there tonight and she hugged on him hard as they shared a deep insight with the power of words. He got up to sing next. He was the life of the party, with his great size and gravelly voice roughly singing with all his might about being a "plastic doll girl." Gentle hated to follow such an act when she was called up next.

Tonight she sought solace in Bon Jovi's "Bed of Roses" and completely lost herself to the desire of love lost and sought, found and lost and forever wanting to just adore one and be adored in return. At the end of the song, she vaguely heard the cheers and acclamations, as she carefully tried not to stagger back to her stool by the bar. Her whole body tingled and shook in an afterglow of ecstasy that thrilled her whenever she performed in full truth.

Her phone barked again and she cleared her mind to focus on a reply. She almost considered tossing him completely aside, it was a pointless friendship after all, one that she didn't understand. But, Gentle acknowledged just how much comfort he always brought to her heart and knew she needed his simple friendship. That's all he ever offered her anyway. She made a vague response about how she loved singing and would probably go home soon, lying, but not knowing what else to do in that moment.

Instead she finished her soda and flirted shamelessly with her forbidden fruit. He returned the favor eagerly and then walked her to her car in the dark parking lot.

Driving home in the clear moonlight she was nearly giddy with emotion, but not in a good way. The Siren had had her meal of sweet kisses in the dark and complained of needing more, but Gentle had learned to manage her better than in the past. She fled for home and found peace and safety flood her soul as the golden light over the garage welcomed her back to her treasured farm.

She knew that there was no judgment waiting inside, no matter what happened, her new found sister welcomed her always, even if she was sound asleep right now. They would reconnect the next evening when their work schedules allowed and Gentle could find wisdom and clarity from Mercy's objective and pragmatic view. She needed Mercy's sisterhood as much as Mercy needed hers in the grief.

Gentle smiled up at Luna's fullness and breathed deep releasing the passion in her own heart that threatened to drown. There was a sudden howl from the gully to the left and Gentle looked into the dark clear night.

A pair of yellow canine eyes blinked slowly through the underbrush and Gentle froze in wonder. She leaned forward and shifted to a form she'd never moved in the physical world so openly before. The white lioness stalked slowly toward the underbrush and sniffed the air. The wolf stepped out only so far as to allow his nose to draw near her and catch her full scent. Suddenly he took off, howling in the single song of a lone hunter and Gentle shivered back to human form standing by the mud porch door, pausing before entering.

"How beautiful," was all she whispered.

Gentle brings forth the music from within.

Chapter 10

The blank wall stared at her.

It was singing, but she couldn't make out the tune quite yet. She laid out the old, discarded tubs of paint she had freely picked up from the waste department's chemical exchange. There was quite a unique combination of colors. The plastic floor covering beckoned to be speckled and with brush in hand, Gentle began as she usually did, with the black outlining.

There wasn't a single drop of Aboriginal blood in her veins, in fact she was only second and third generation (British descent) Australian, but there was something about being born and raised in the Great South Land that imbued the nature of her beauty and her terror in that wide brown land,

"for me," sighed the Auzzie born girl, reciting to herself the love of the Sunburnt Country. She looked again at the song that seeped forth from the dry wall seeing both what was and what would manifest. She smiled wondering where the Aboriginal influence came from. Shrugging with artistic surrender, Gentle just kept painting.

One of the key tools she had learned to use during her walkabout for healing was that of the creativity that surged within. She had suppressed much of it all her life for various reasons, mostly that she was too poor to play with such mediums and didn't think she had enough talent to be worthy of actual education in such. But, thus was her blood that Gentle discovered if she did not spend time creating every day then the excess of such juices would swirl within and turn toxic, causing all manner of mental distress and behavioral ailments that is was just better to let go of the excuses and just do what she did. It didn't have to look like anyone else's and in fact rarely did she do anything the same way as anyone else.

Gentle didn't just walk to the beat of her own drum she danced, played, conducted and made the very instruments of her own orchestra that continually played forth from within. The wall of her apartment was the current manifestation of this song.

The sleigh bells that hung on the front door knob upstairs jangled and Gentle heard the heavy footsteps of Mercy returning from work. She covered the tub that she was using, rinsed her brushes and made her way upstairs to attend to her sister.

Mercy was crashed on her bed, red faced and puffy eyed. The exhaustion of insomnia, grief and plodding work, blanketed her soul as if to suffocate.

Gentle asked softly from the door way,

"Will they give you the time off?"

Mercy sighed in resignation,

"Yeah, but she says if I can come back sooner that she needs me."

"No." said Gentle emphatically. "You need to stop awhile and let the grief travel through you so you can journey on." Gentle's heart ached to see Mercy's suffering. There were no words of consolation or advice for comfort that could possibly explain or lessen the cutting reality of her loss. Even Gentle didn't think she could bare such a permanent loss to love. She knew loss, but never the eternal permanence of death in one so intrinsically apart of her inner soul as a Partner.

Gentle thought of her friend and sister's love. Quess had been a troubled and misunderstood man, but how he had loved his lady Mercy.

"Do you know what one of my favorite memories of him is?" Gentle sat on the edge of the bed by Mercy's curled up feet and recalled, "Quess was running around, spinning in his usual chaos," Mercy's eyes smiled a memory that didn't quite make it to her mouth. Gentle continued, "he bustled past us then stopped mid walk, turned, looked at me, pointed to you and said, 'that woman right there is the love of my life and I love her more than anything in the world.' He then smacked a kiss on your forehead and spun on again."

Mercy's eyes welled and she whispered,

"I don't remember that."

"Well I do, very clearly." Gentle laid a hand on Mercy's leg. "He loved you so much."

Mercy voiced her concern,

"But I can't help thinking it was my fault. I let him spin out of control. I could have put a stop to it."

"No, my dear sister," Gentle consoled, "You gave him the freedom of unconditional love to just be who he was where everyone else would have caged him."

"But to what end?" Mercy cried.

Gentle spoke the wisdom that she and her sister had concluded in earlier rational studies of the facts on Quess' life,

"Quess had such darkness buried in him that turned toxic deep inside from years of suppression. His darkness was not his doing. It was random tragedy that was left unattended and misunderstood for forty years. Such 'demons' or whatever you want to label them as, are not let loose lightly but they WILL surface." Gentle looked out the window to the setting sun feeling a familiar pinch in her own soul rise as was her habit at twilight. "It is what we do with our demons when they confront us that makes all the difference."

"I just couldn't." Mercy sighed. "I couldn't lock him up like his family always did." She sat up, "I had to let him spin it out."

"And there," pointed Gentle, "is where you gave him the freedom he had never known before. You gave him the chance to open up the caged beast and try to make peace with him."

Mercy remembered the horror of those last weeks,

"But the monster was too strong. He'd been buried for too long."

Gentle concluded,

"No one could have foreseen or been able to stay back such darkness."

Mercy cuddled her pillow. She knew Quess was gone. The old man hawk had flown south to attend to the needs of his children that still careened off the edge of grief and heartache, arguments and misunderstandings. So now the sky was empty over Springhill Farm and a dire wolf howled in the winds of loneliness, combining all their cries that haunted the filling moon.

A lookout to sea crashed over by the tumultuous waves.

Chapter 11

Mercy opened up what she'd been holding back since the last morning,

"I dreamed of him again, only this time, I think it was the last."

"How so?" asked Gentle.

"We were driving in his jeep and he said to me, 'I only have as long as this drive.'" Mercy allowed a trickle down her cheek to fall unchecked. "We talked about a few different things but then he said he had to go back to his family for a while." Mercy drew in a deep breath, "I think his daughter needs him more than I do right now."

Gentle looked out the big bedroom window to the clear, empty sky,

"Maybe it's just for a season. The spirit world doesn't operate that same way our physical world does."

Mercy looked to her sister and said,

"I just block most of it out. I don't really want to know, except for what God brings to me."

Gentle smiled, "It's so cool to me that you have re-found your faith. Even though it looks different to mine, I hear the truth and that is still the same."

"Yeah, I found my faith when I was ignoring it with Quess, a truly profane man who found his soul more akin to Druids than Christians."

Gentle offered a theory,

"If Elohim is indeed the one true God who created the world and has angels that do His bidding and dark angels that fight against Him, it makes sense to me that all things created for His glory should be an intrinsic part of Himself, thus, perhaps, nature is not so separate and the physical world just might be riddled with spiritual things we cannot see, unless we choose to."

Gentle looked out onto the naked back yard and saw with spirit eyes what others missed. She smiled at the children playing tag, the fae folk dancing in the lights and shadows, and the forgotten souls wandering in search of closure. She let a tear fall wondering why so many still wandered the earth after living privileges had been revoked.

Mercy recognized the look in her sister's eye and asked,

"Is the paddock full again tonight?"

Gentle moved away from the window,

"It is loud. The full moon waxes and I have no idea why they gather here."

Mercy followed her into the kitchen to scrounge for food,

"Maybe they are just here because you sense them."

"Well, I don't know what to do with them, so I just point out the way home and tell them to go."

Gentle recited her motto,

"Nothing can separate us from the love of God; neither life or death, and not principalities or dark powers. Love covers a multitude of sins and while there may be only one way to God the Father; Immanuel, God with us, stands on an open hill top and there is no one way to Him." She looked out the big, bay window and willed her spirit voice call across the crowded empty fields,

"Go home," she called, "why wait here?"

The same answer replied as always,

"The Timing."

The timing indeed, it seemed everyone's lives and deaths had their own personal clock. Gentle was too often greatly impatient with hers. This clear sensing of things unseen was still new to her and she felt very much like a toddler on fat new legs, bumbling around, falling down, and trying not to get into too much mischief.

She'd made mistakes as she tried to discern what she sensed. It was all so confusing, especially when spirit visions evolved in the physical world. That kind of cross over caused all manner of alarming opportunities for mistakes. Like the time when Gentle had foreseen a champion coming. She knew for two days that a Champion was on his way and that he would arrive in a leather suit of armor riding upon a stead of chrome.

So when someone completely unexpected turned up in just that manner and was there for Mercy and not her, Gentle had still gotten her lonely wires all crossed and mistook him for her lost hero returned. He resembled Beloved so very much, that familiar military air of command. She saw her lost warrior in so many men that passed by her life. It seemed the more she tried to forget him, the more he showed up.

The aftermath of her jumping to conclusions had very nearly been disastrous, but for the acceptance of large souls who allowed for weirdness and didn't rely on social expectations to rule their reactions. Gentle shuddered in embarrassment.

Elohim usually had her walk only one step at a time and she had difficulty not running ahead without a clue as to where she was going. It led her to amazing places full of the humiliation of open vulnerability where her soul was laid bare to be poked and prodded and studied by anyone passing by.

Most chose to harden their hearts against such raw exposure, but not so was Gentle allowed. Elohim required she keep her heart soft, tender and thus, often bleeding because in doing so, perhaps one other might recognize their own heart in her reflection and a bridge of communion would be created. Communion was the ultimate Divine desire that always came at the cost of sacrifice. Yet, always, worth every drop of pain that sweated from the hearts of those who built bridges and connected lives.

Not even the World Wide Web could imitate the intricate wonder of human connection. So, Gentle maintained her bleeding heart and was enriched by every life she came across as a result. Who else would she have the privilege to love she wondered?

That night in her meditations, on her Island, Gentle drew a map. She rolled it up into a glass bottle and tossed it out to sea from off the edge of the peninsular.

"Here is the map to my island, my Captain, whoever you are." She thought she saw sails in the distance, "come and find me." Gentle raised her voice and sang to the crashing waves that sucked over the surging tide of rock infested waters.

In the distance, a Jolly Rodger frantically flapped in a coming storm. He heard a whisper,

"I cannot love you fully. Go find someone who can," so the sails billowed full speed ahead.

The type of car Gentle dreamed of owning someday.

Chapter 12

Mercy rose up in her days of rest and worked from dawn to dusk to alleviate the torment of grief. There was never a moment of nothing to do in the life of a farm girl. Not only did she have her new farm to attend to the mowing, caring for horse fencing and coral cleaning, but there was still her past home that needed purging.

The home she had moved her mother out of was the one they had lived in for thirty years and thirty years of farm accumulation was something that only diligence of the obsessive kind would ever be able to conquer.

Every room, every inch of the yard, and every out building overflowed with the loving attentions of, "I can't throw it out. We might need that someday."

Mercy cleaned with her own tears. The purging and the cleansing of that physical home did much to revert within and allow for the purging and the cleansing of her soul.

Gentle watched Mercy's frenzy. She wanted to help and offered what she could but seemed constricted in her own life and unable to reach out very far in any kind of legitimate assistance. She knew her sister ached and there was little to be done but to wait. But the waiting caused its own restlessness that needed attending to, on its own terms.

The very air was restless. Her mood was restless. The siren within wrestled against her.

There was nothing distracting on television and she had not enough money to be distracted at the theater, so in her distraction, Gentle sought to expend the energies that surged within. There was no karaoke tonight instead live music at her local pub offered the chance through noise volume to cancel out the loudness within.

Her phone barked. The siren's teeth snapped. Tonight was no night to allow her near such a sweet young friend.

"I'm headed out to the bar a while, driving in a bit," was the only text she could squeeze out of her clenching claws.

"You seem to go out a lot." He replied, undaunted.

A mild twinge of guilt panged and she settled slightly,

"Well, I like to hang out with friends." But the siren pushed for more honesty, "and I get restless."

"Restless? Are you ok?"

"Yes I'm FINE." She snapped like a typical woman with absolutely nothing fine about her. The siren warned, "You shouldn't provoke if you don't want to get bitten."

There was only a brief pause before he responded,

"You know you don't have to worry about me. I can handle more than you might think."

"No." and Gentle almost threw her phone into her pocket depths before the siren could coax him out further for her tasting.

The screaming in her head pressed on the accelerator and Gentle fought to maintain legal and safe driving skills. She focused on "Invictus",

"I am the master of my fate / I am the captain of my soul"

The facilitations she had practiced so deftly settled the squabble within.

But Murmurs was alive and her growling soul chuffed to hear the shenanigans. It was with some disappointment that she sauntered into the bar and saw that everyone was either her own age or older.

"Poop, old farts."

She promptly laughed at herself. Age may have counted the experience of all those here tonight, but there wasn't an aged soul there. Some were perhaps ancient or timeless, but as she looked about, she saw only the vibrant souls of those seeking to live fully despite the aging cage of the physical.

"Old age seems so much younger each day I approach it." Gentle thought.

She wasn't really old. She was only coming up on her forty-second birthday and was geekfully delighted to be so akin to the "Answer to the meaning of Life the Universe and Everything" (as Douglas Adams would put it). But as she felt more like a twenty-three year old, the forties seemed still hilariously far away.

She sat at the bar and ordered her extravagant glass of water and turned to listen to the band. They were pretty good.

A couple of tipsy gals were dancing and beckoned her to join. Gentle didn't like dancing in bars. Her movements to music were more suited to an extravagant Goth dance floor than just the tame amblings of the Local. She declined but made friends with them anyway and they introduced her to their entire group. The evening danced about her as new people were met and re-met.

One gentleman, his name was Justus, wore the colors of retired seamanship and she couldn't help herself being drawn into conversation. He wasn't typically one she'd have paid too much mind to, but he was kind, and noble in his perusal of conversation so she granted her ear and received his attentions generously. The offer to go for a ride on his bike and then a drive in his sports car cinched it though. It wasn't just any sports car. Gentle didn't care much for flashy toys like that. But he had the one car that Gentle dreamed of owning herself, so of course she would love to go for a drive.

The evening was blissful and innocent, he was a lovely gentleman. He even asked for a parting kiss. His confession of having another love jarred a little, but in her blindness, she believed the traditional lie about sailors and all their port lovers as if that was somehow acceptable, just because it was typical. He was to take her for a ride tomorrow afternoon.

That next day was a whirlwind of joy, connection and bliss on the back of a Harley. He took her for a ride and carried her to such thrills as she had only ever dreamed. They were like kindred souls that missed each other far too long and in finally finding such connection the fireworks were brilliant. In retrospect, Gentle only wished she had seen what hazardous firepower was required to set those colors ablaze.

When she floated across the back yard to her basement home the next day, she didn't even hear the deep growl coming from the gully's underbrush.

Surrounded by, and basking in nature's light.

Chapter 13

Her boys were the joy of her soul.

The first decade of their lives had been regrettably tumultuous. Their mother stayed with them at home, but for brief attempts to find employ for extra distraction and finances. Yet their mother was increasingly distorted from a darkness within that never found place or time for healing from without. As a result, those three precious angels grew up knowing their mommy was just sick and needed to go spend time away, in hospital, or in other places to help her get better. When the final shoe was dropped and divorce was laid out their hearts shattered as she left.

From an outward perspective, a woman leaving her home, leaving everything there, taking not even any remuneration for the split, it might easily appear to be simple abandonment. And thus was the misunderstanding that was allowed to breed in the minds of any who watched from a distance.

However the mother, who had spent thirteen years living, eating, sleeping and breathing her family, could no longer hold back the dark that shattered her soul and only watched helplessly as it attacked her husband. She knew the only way to keep her sons safe from long term harm, was to leave and take the poison within as far away as she could.

Gentle had given up. For six years she had fought on the battlefield of mental and emotional disorder. Nothing helped.

The medications only caused the electrons firing inside to be dulled thus slugging the creative flow that was her life blood. Professionals diligently sought ways to fix her, not one of them asking what was going on in the back ground, what was hidden behind the innocent evil picket fence. She was the monster, everyone else her victim. No one could figure out how to fix her. Gentle believed the lie that she needed fixing. So, when the fight was too overwhelming, she gave up.

For almost three years she allowed herself to be tossed about in the wind. Following whatever party needed a designated driver. She was the one to call. She would do whatever you needed her too. She would do whatever you asked. Many asked too much.

One morning, Gentle woke up and recognized the grime she was living in as that deep place underneath rock bottom. She looked up at Elohim, as she often did, and asked,

"Can I please come home now?"

Elohim withdrew the arm that had been extended out against her, holding her at bay, allowing the wiles of the dark conglomeration to have its way with her. She didn't understand why. She couldn't see beyond her own eyelashes so she knew there was no hope for her understanding, but now, this morning, she sensed somehow,

"Can I come home?"

He engulfed her in His love. His tears, at her heartache and wretched wounded soul, washed over her and she blinked in the freshness of hope. Looking up she saw it was a long way up just to rock bottom again and from there . . . she dare not even think.

In that first week of surrender, laying under the covers of her cold winter room after having spent her first moments of waking paying toll to the porcelain gods for no reason other than excess stress and "severe anxiety" (as was the medical diagnosis), Gentle clasped her old bible to her chest. She had not even the ability to open and read it, but here with her arms around the big, clumsy book, she felt Elohim embrace her and hope etched upon her for the first time in a very, very long time.

She drifted away even further from her sons, never leaving them fully. Always doing all she could to connect with them on a regular basis through technology. Some days, that was all she could do. Then after a space of healing, after moving to a place full of love and acceptance that allowed her the chance to breathe and clear her head a little more, Gentle realized the gift she had been given.

"I have so absolutely nothing right now that I have to start all over again. I can re-start life anywhere I want, anyway I want, and anyhow I want. Where will I re-begin?"

That is when, with the assistance of family, she returned to her homeland Down Under and began her walkabout for healing. She continued to keep in touch with her sons, growing stronger each month in a typical two steps forward, and one step back. Her online friendships developing a depth that gave buoyancy to her spirit allowing more and more healing light to come filtering through the dissipating dark.

She even had the privilege through random interaction on the train to and from work to connect with another soul of light and that friendship electrified her healing journey even more, giving a powerful boost to it. Her evenings spent laughing with Lexa, eating good food, and walking along the beach, taking in the sounds of waves and good music meant more to her than even she realized at the time.

Gentle spent hours immersing herself in the natural world of the Cronulla beaches. The wind, the waves, the rocks, the sand, occasionally getting in the freezing water, but mostly just being a part of life and allowing that to intoxicate her, all worked together melting away the disordered dread of hopelessness.

When she finally returned across the sea, for a brief visit to see her precious sons again, the strength of her soul had lifted enough that she could no longer bear the thought of ever leaving them, so with parting plane ticket discarded, she turned her rental car around and returned to stay. That night, waiting for a last faithful friend to offer temporary shelter, Gentle smiled at the adventure that was about to happen. With no work, no transportation, and no place to live . . . what could possibly go wrong?

As much as you might think and less than you would ever believe.

Gentle was excited as she cleaned her basement apartment. They were staying with her for a full week this summer break, her sons: Peaz, Manson and Sirreh. Her biggest plan for them was that they just get to explore the farm and be young teenage boys.

A drunken Bumblebee feeds on a golden pear.

Chapter 14

On the morning that Gentle was to pick her sons up for their farm holiday, she stepped out into the blazing sunshine and the customary mooings that greeted her appearance. She smiled and breathed deeply. The apple trees were dumping fresh loads of fruit on the ground each morning and Gentle was spending a couple hours each day just gathering for cows, horses and inside cooking.

Mercy had batches of dried apples on racks, jars of apple butter boiled on the stove and apple pies to share with the farmer who rented their fields. The pear tree was beginning to drop as well and both girls loved sucking the sweet meat off the fruit.

Gentle knelt in the grass after tossing apples to cows and horses, gathering the pears in the mid-morning sun. There was a glow humming off the ground as the green grass snuggled with the golden orbs of heavily scented flesh. And, yes, it really was that clichéd and idyllic. The humming was attributed to the multitude of bees that buzzed drunkenly from sweet meat to sweet meat. There were honey bees, yellow jackets, and bumbles.

Gentle knelt quietly, carefully picking up each pear and slowly dislodging the buzzy workers while softly singing to them. She giggled in delight as they staggered across her fingers, dozy and drunk on the sweet nectar. Most of them just sat and washed their faces while she studied their pretty fuzzy profiles on her thumb nail.

She heard a happy yip that barked up out of the gully and thought it was her phone at first, but then the rush of fur dashing under cover out of sight made her smile. Above, Luna was smiling down, plump and nearly full again in the clear blue sky. Gentle longed to see the wolf up close. She strained her neck to see if he might venture out, but he was off pouncing after some shadow that needed chasing as he set watch over his territory.

Zoe whinnied at her so the last of the over ripe and rotting pears were dumped at her feet. Codger cantered up and that caught the attention of both Shyner and Macro. Gentle turned to see both 1200 pound geldings galloping up the hill toward her. She stood her ground and demanded they calm down.

"No dashing about when I'm in here with you, thank you very much."

Shyner skittered his feet out slowing down, but Macro had the wind up regions of his anterior and pushed his way into the crowd. There was an equestrian jostling and Gentle was bustled by tails and mass muscle.

"Oi!" She yelled, landing a smack on Macro's shoulder, "quit being a dingbat while I'm in here." Macro was too wired up on sunshine and the smell of pears to realize with whom he was dealing and continued stomping and demanding his way.

Gentle ceased being that of her first name and the essence of her middle name burst forth from her lungs as she yelled,

"I said quit it!" She clapped her hands together to part the stomping hooves from about her perimeters. The heard scattered.

Macro bucked as he demanded the heard follow his lead and kicked out against the littlest in the field, deftly clipping Gentle Warrior sharply on her hip with his hoof.

"Oh, HELL NO, you just didn't!" Gentle glared after the galloping gelding as he took off across the field. "Oh Hell No you Will NOT!" she repeated.

With a determination larger than any of the equestrians in the paddock, Gentle limped on her swelling and bruised hip toward the coral entrance. She kept a large stick there to whack the post as a call to home each evening when she needed the horses in for feeding. But, now she had a mind to whack something more akin to horse hair and butt.

She stalked out into the paddock, still limping and the gelding could smell her fury. He kept himself cantering at a distance but ended up cornered by her determination and soundly sorry in the end. His ears, also, received a thrashing as all the exuberance of her vocal collective trounced his behavior. The neighbors became apprised of the situation. He cowered before his Warrior, head bent in regret, backing up as she taught him with ironic exampling how to be of gentle character despite his self-absorbed dumb-battery.

She stood strong and quiet before the mighty gelding with large stick resting against her shoulder. He bowed his head again and sniffed at the hand she held out to him. Slowly he stepped in toward her and nuzzled against her sorrowfully. Gentle scratched his chin and returned the cuddles, kissing his soft muzzle. They would be best of companions from now on.

Gentle then limped up through the parking lot toward her car. She smiled, rubbing her hip, loving the strength that farm life had empowered within her. Her sons could learn a lot from this way of life.

As she drove down the road to fetch her boys, a dual canine audience applauded her from over in the gully. The little red fox watched with wide eyes communing in wonder to his Wolfy neighbor. They had been watching the whole event. The wolf smiled too, howling in pride as if to say,

"That's my gurl."

Summer sleepover with the box cradle and fold out couch beds.

Chapter 15

"Foop" went the feather tick. Manson had flopped upon the old, hand stuffed feather mattress cover that LaMa and her mother had made when she was a little girl. He sighed in rest as the sides puffed up about him, but then groaned loudly as his dearly beloved younger bother, Sirreh, flopped on top of him. Peaz giggled and clapped his hands gleefully, tossing himself onto the brother pile. There was another muffled moaning from the midst of philadelphic feathers and the giggling began. It didn't come from the pile, but rather from the mema who watched over her sons.

Gentle embraced her boys en masse as they rolled in the cuddles of feathers, giggling together. Dinner was done and beds were being made with blankets galore on the fold out couches. Sirreh had claimed the great wooden box for his cradle and Gentle giggled telling him that a hundred years ago, its use was for boiling pig carcasses but it was well clean now and made a great coffin-like nest for him upon piles of pillows and blankets. The pre-teen loved it.

As Gentle was a firm believer in bedtime stories, no matter what age the listener, so she allowed the boys to settle themselves and then began the secret journey with them she had longed to undertake; reading her first novel to them. Each night that week they would meet in bed to hear the tale of magic, terror, fantasy, impossible sports, and personal choices in a world of wonder that was surprisingly close to home. The scribe hoped her sons enjoyed the telling for they were her beta audience.

Sirreh begged she continue one more chapter with sleepy eyes but sensible Manson agreed sleep was in order. Peaz was already snoring from under his collection of stuffed friends. Gentle kissed each of her boys more proud of who they were in themselves than anything she could create. She kept one light low so they could see to the bathroom in the unfamiliar surrounding should they have need and then retreated to her own private chambers.

Kneeling again before her bed, she quickly dabbed a drop of holy water and anointing oil to ease the connection of her prayers. She was full of grateful thanks and praise that she could spend such delightful moments with her sons. Her love overflowed in her joy.

Immanuel called her to use some of that overflow for an impossible mission.

"I want you to tell him I AM still loves him."

Gentle turned to look over her shoulder and saw the dark one approach, yet keep at a distance. She looked back to her Lord with questioning in her eyes, asking only that she be granted the ability to see with that same Divine vision. Looking again, to her mission, she walked toward the dark Coyote King. He growled his greeting,

"What do you want?"

"He still loves you. Won't you come home?"

The Coyote just stared at her in sarcastic disbelief,

"Really?" He adjusted his glasses pushing a middle finger up his nose to restore visual balance and display his mood. "Aren't you bible scholars supposed to know the ending?"

Gentle looked on the face of darkness. She saw the determined hopelessness, the bitterness, the pride, the disgust. Then she saw him how he was, once, many ages ago,

"You were so beautiful."

He adjusted his outward fashion and appeared before her with such glorious attraction that even Gentle's heart eyes gasped a little.

"I can be as beautiful as you need me to be." He approached her slowly with sweet seduction. Tenderly, he ran his fingers down her cheek and drew his sweet lips close to hers.

Gentle saw him as Immanuel did and allowed the tears of genuine love to trickle down her face. The dark king leaned in as if to kiss the trail of tears and Gentle lifted her own hand toward his face, he flinched slightly. She placed her hand fully upon his cheek seeking his eyes for any Truth within, but he recoiled as the contact of her hand on his face seared and burned like a hot iron.

Backing up he swore vehemently, but Gentle pursued reaching out to him,

"Nothing need separate you from real Love. Won't you come home?"

A barrage of language spewed forth from the darkness of his pride and he fled from her determined to return the burning to anywhere in her life that he could reach.

Immanuel, ever her back up and support, placed a pierced hand on her shoulder and whispered,

"He will never return to Us."

Gentle leaned on her comfort,

"Just because I know that, doesn't mean I'll ever stop telling him how much You Love."

"Never stop telling them, Gentle. Never stop telling them how much they are loved." The Voice implored her with an,

"AMEN."

Gentle snuggled under her feather comforter in the sweet cool of her basement bedroom. With her head heavy in the drowsiness of deep meditation, she offered up a prayer and determined to love her best, wherever she was able.

She answered her networking messages quickly, returning the cute puppy photo that waited in her inbox with a grumpy kitty picture that always made her giggle, then she texted a brief prayer to her new friend Justus and he agreed to catch up with her again after her boys were returned to their home.

Gentle looked eagerly for the dawn to rise and the playtime with her sons to dance into full swing. Tomorrow they were to go horse riding. Everyone would love that.

Peaz tells a tale of the Wolf King.

Chapter 16

Prayers in the dark before the dawn were blissful again that morning, and after dozing briefly, Gentle's world rocked softly in her waking to the sound track of quiet nattering and Lego clattering. She smiled and stretched big, listening to her boys waking. The stairs creaked as toes tipped up to the bathroom and the kitchen floor greeted the hungry fasters back from their night's break. Snuggling briefly with sorrow at missing these little things in her daily life, Gentle then left such thoughts under her pillow and rose up with a smile to embrace the present day of joy.

The three young men stood in the paddock mildly unsure of themselves, but eager to try something new. Manson was most eager and held the reigns of the complacent Codger while Mercy buckled up the saddle. Peaz, Sirreh, and Gentle sat under the walnut tree in the warm breeze waiting their turn. There was a scuttle in the distance and a flash of red as the cheeky fox dashed under cover.

Sirreh asked,

"Did you hear what he said?"

Peaz sang to himself,

"Ring-ding-ding-ding-dingeringeding."

The family on the hill giggled.

Sirreh said,

"You should put him in your book, mom. He could be the bad Red Fox King."

Gentle looked into the ravine with distance in her eyes musing,

"The Red Fox King of the Brownies is not really evil but quite naughty and Regent of the mischievous horde of pranksters."

"Pixie pranksters?" asked Manson, having just climbed up into the saddle.

"Brownies and Pixies are quite different tribes of fae." Gentle tried to recall the education she'd received while reading the much celebrated English author Enid Blyton. "Pixies have a more deliberate delight to them. Brownies, I believe, usually have a darker intent."

Manson suggested,

"Perhaps they are the ones who steal socks from the dryer as socrifices to the laundry gods?"

They all laughed and Manson reined Codger in behind Mercy and Shyner as they took a leisurely lap around the paddock.

"Mummy," Peaz asked, flapping his hands in excitement, "did you hear my story about the Wolf King?"

"The Wolf King?" Gentle tried not to sound too intrigued, "do tell." She then leaned in to cuddle Sirreh, who was flopped on her lap as they listened to the excited and random ramblings of Peaz' storytelling.

The warm wind carried heavy summer rest in its breath and meandered past the riders then down into the hollow ravine.

The Red Fox yipped in an excited whisper to his neighbor,

"A king? I get to be a king? That's so exciting. I never thought I could be a king, I mean I'd considered a regent, or even governor's office before, but I never, ever thought I might be able to be a king. What would the Coyotes say? A King, the Red fox King of the Brownies!"

He was suddenly silenced by a massive wolf paw laid carefully and heavily upon his head.

The Red Fox blinked under his squished and wrinkled brow watching the family on the hill top. He mumbled with mild disgust through his snout buried in the dirt,

"I might not invite you to tea anymore if this is how you're going to treat my hospitality." His nose sunk deeper under the furry weight.

"Hush," The deep voice of dire Wolfy-ness spoke, "I'm listening to the story."

"Ah, yes, yes, of course, the story. Excellent teller that . . ."

The massive wolf growled and the little red fox bit his tongue in silence.

Peaz continued to dance across the hilltop pulling details from every story he'd ever seen or heard and gathered them all together in his own cooking pot of Tale. The wind carried his voice all the way across the fields to the dark Kingdom Gates.

Prince Don Coyote heard the whispers and skittered off to the central inked glade where he came to a panting stop entreating audience with his brother King.

"What is it," Yawned the comfortable ruler?

"There's another king, sire," The anxious canine warned.

"Not of any consequence, brother." He sucked his teeth, "not of any consequence."

Prince Don cleared his throat,

"But Gentle's oldest tells of him."

A low growl at the mention of her name reverberated through the hall. He began pacing and waved his paw at the empty air as invisible plans and strategies slowly became visible in a displaced war room that now wavered into this particular dimensional space. The King studied his preparations and said,

"I know of no such king."

There was a jostling in the corner when a band of large sentries argued amongst themselves.

The Coyote King snapped,

"If you have something to bring to my attention, then do so."

A skinny guard was tossed forward and he stuttered with a guilty admission,

"I have seen one such a wolf."

The Coyote slunk on all fours and circled the stammering soldier interrogating him,

"Where?"

The victim blinked,

"In the gully by the farm house."

"When?"

The victim swallowed,

"Yesterday."

The King slunk onto his throne feigning camaraderie,

"And what was this little wolf doing so near the farm house, chasing chickens?" There was an obligatory snickering from the other occupants of the dark glade.

"Oh, he's not little," blurted the victim, "he's enormous, as wolves go, quite the dire wolf, actually." He looked around for back up from the others, but only silence greeted him.

The King leaned back picking his teeth, relaying the information,

"So what you're telling me is that you saw a foreigner in my kingdom with the appearance of a potential threat, and yet not only did you not arrest him and bring him here to be questioned, but you also didn't tell me about this encounter?" The King stared at his victim, "Am I missing anything?"

In a desperate attempt to save the last shred of his life, the coyote's victim vomited the remains of his truth,

"He chased me!"

"Excuse me?" the king would not allow such insubordination.

"I was watching him from the shadows while he was keeping an eye on Gentle when he disappeared. The next thing I knew, he was rushing me from behind and chased me all the way back here."

"Oh, you poor thing," Prince Don was all condolences. "You had to run all the way back to our gates with the big bad wolf snapping at your heels did you?" There was some muttered chuckling emanating from the dark corners and the other soldiers readied their taste buds.

"Yes," pouted the witless victim.

"Thus leading him to our 'secret' entrance?" The Regal Coyote stepped down from his throne, claws clinking in shimmering deadliness. "Well then, let me relieve you of your distress and stupidity." He slashed with instant reflexes and forgot with instant carelessness that the victim had even existed. Prince Don directed the rabble in the corner to devour the carcass as they wished.

The Coyote King used his blood dipped claws to draw an 'x' and circle it on his map. He snarled intoxicated by death,

"This could be interesting." He smiled, liking his paws clean.

A Moonbeam Faery Path glitters upon the way of hope.

Chapter 17

Food was eaten, drinks were mixed and drunk (of the chocolate milk kind), laughter was plentiful, adventure was sought and found, and much love was nurtured. All in all, it was a wonderful week of simple farm living for a family full of hope and new beginnings.

The early teen boys especially loved the bedtime story their mema read to them each night. She had longed to share the tale she'd been creating for nearly a decade. There was a whole universe, populated and wondrous, that she couldn't wait to share with the rest of the world. To talk about, laugh and cry with the heroines, fight the villains, cheer on the underdog and debate over the choices each made in their own hearts. Her son's loved it and Gentle cherished their delight.

But after her full week was up, she pulled out of their driveway and turned the radio up loudly.

A song came on that reminded her too clearly of loneliness and how her heart still yearned for a long lost Beloved. She knew not if he lived, or if he had died a hero's death. She would never know. So to ease her aching soul, she wished for another Captain to take his place. Perhaps she could steal one away from his ocean. Perhaps one would make for land and find home upon her shores, keeping her comforted in all the night watches.

With a twinge of guilt she sent a text to Justus.

Even as she waited for his response she questioned why she sought to relieve her aching heart in places where pain only seemed to thrive? 'Because she was human' was the only answer she could ignore as she continued on her set path. She was determined to be loved, no matter how much it hurt in the end. Her impatience knew no bounds.

The phone barked and she left it where it was concentrating on her driving. But when the text ding from Justus sang in her ears, she pulled over into a parking lot to arrange for another meeting by the river.

Summer was dreamy by the river and possibilities were endless.

Justus was open to receiver her and their connection was powerful and instant. Neither could explain how they connected so fully and so quickly. Their conversations were spiritual and learned, both having a past of study. Their agreement on foundations and core beliefs were as one and their kisses . . . oh, the kisses . . . .

It was a summer romance of epic proportion. "Amazing" was all Gentle could say with her glow burning in blinding brilliance as she recalled the day's events to her sister Mercy. Mercy took to calling him "the Amazing Justus" but her tone was more sarcastic than admiring.

Justus met Mercy when he stopped by the farm for a quick visit. He was as much enamored with Gentle as she was with him. But, Mercy took an immediate dislike to him and warned her sister of her uneasiness at such exuberant happiness. Gentle took note of her sister's wisdom. She didn't discard it, but attended to her cautions, yet she was so happy that she clung to the moment just hoping with expected dread that she might hold on as long as she could.

As Justus rode his chrome away, the equestrian herd demanded food, so Gentle floated down to the coral moving to where she could not see the other side of the farm.

The gully on the far edges held shadows that lengthened in the twilight and as the sailor rode by a sudden rush startled and he swerved to avoid the shadow. Speeding up, sensing something unseen, he shook his head in the wind trying to find clarity in the confusing waves that crashed in his own heart.

The wolf chased him all the way down the road barking ferociously and howled loudly in defense of his territory at the crest. Satisfied that potential threats had been discarded for the moment, he trotted happily, tongue out panting, all the way back down to his gully.

As Gentle curled to sleep in her feathered bed that night, a sorrowful howl pierced the night and a darkness crept in where it was not welcome. A weakness in the walls had been found and the arrow launched. Gentle tossed in her dreaming.

It was a dark night on the island and the white lioness prowled the hilltop. Pacing back and forth she watched the beaches below. The moon shone in brilliant silver and the fae path twinkled upon the resting waters of the sea out past the crashing waves that ringed her fortress.

With a flying leap, the lioness pounced upon the moonbeam transforming into the trio of sisters that inhabited the lands of subconscious safety. They climbed upon the silver path seeking the heights of understanding. Hope and dread mingled slippery under foot and many a wing beating was necessary to aid in the climb. The clouds settled about them and another dimension opened up ushering visitations from a dark companion of long ago.

Hard and cold plate-armor clinked in the air as the Siren braced for attack and faery dust swirled as the delicate one prepared also. Gentle stood her ground between the two watching warily as he approached.

"Good even, lover." He crooned.

"I am and never was yours to love. What interest do you have with me?" Gentle was not afraid.

He smirked,

"Well, I never loved you, but you know that." He chuckled, "You of all creatures should know I am incapable of such, hey pretty one?" He tapped the faery girl's chin, and she looked sadly into his eyes.

The Siren dropped her spear closer toward his person in silence.

"Ahh, yes, the guardian," He circled the warrior, "you're so strong and deadly," he stepped up to whisper into her ear from behind, "unless you know where to find the chink." He licked her neck and she shuddered.

Gentle took hold of all her hands singing clearly to the Light in the darkness.

"I'm going." He tossed his hands up in the air smirking at the wonder of himself. "I just wanted to visit you again." He leered lustily at the three, "I miss this separation of you."

Gentle lifted her hands in prayer and the three became one again. She stood towering as an Amazon beauty with all three sets of wings billowing out from her back singing her mediations of praise to Elohim.

The darkness left.

Gentle lowered her arms and walked ignorantly past a different pair of carefully hidden yellow blinking eyes watching from the forest shadows. She made her way eagerly to the cabin nestled as a lean-to in the shadow of the Lighthouse. There was comfort in the sight of a great bed in the corner, a constant fire by the hearth and a long wooden table in the center. She was not alone here, there was much comfort awaiting her and she entered her rest looking ahead with open heart, vulnerable and ready for battle.

When she awoke the next day there was a voicemail on her phone from Justus. He requested they talk. There was much heaviness in his voice and Gentle knew the ocean called to this sailor again and even she was not strong enough to hold him back from her, his mistress.

Grace and mercy comes only from the secret places.

Chapter 18

Care you to know the agony, my reader? I step outside this tale for a brief moment to ask if you really want to see the desperation that comes from love given too freely, too quickly, and then torn apart too soon. I do not recommend such uninhibited feelings. Shakespeare warned us of these things years ago. I never really liked the story of Romeo and Juliet. I guess I am lucky no one died a physical death here. But, do you really want to know?

I look back with no regret on those long and drawn out moments, for it was not mercifully done in one instant. Life rarely is merciful. Elohim is merciful. He calls us to be merciful, but we do not live in a merciful world. Ask anyone. I offer mercy and grace because in doing so, I receive the gift of healing into my own soul. Therefore, I will pass over these events and simply say, I am grateful to have loved and been loved.

This grace and mercy comes only from the secret places.

Gentle sat on the paddock hilltop of Springhill Farm under the stars listening to her music. She sang with gusto and poured out her heart in passion, pain, and grateful praise. But, just when she felt loneliest her phone barked. She burst into tears with humble thanks that such a friend could hear her need from so far away. He soothed her sadness, embraced her with his care and let her know she was far from being alone, no matter how far away he was.

"I may only be your friend," he said, "but I am your friend always and I am loyal to the end."

"Manly," texted Gentle (for that was his name), "I have been seeking a true friend all this time and you have always been here for me."

"I always will be." The type relayed

"I need someone I can trust," she whispered. "There is so much more in me, both of dark and light, than I dare not tell anyone."

"I told you once, you needn't worry about me. I can handle more than you might think." He waited a space then continued, "There is more in me than most might guess also."

"Just sit with me?" Gentle asked as she curled on the grass much comforted by his distant presence, and the Wolf in the shadows stepped out to sit by her as a dire gargoyle guarding his sanctuary.

On the Island, Gentle sat with feet dangling over the edge of the peninsular cliff. She looked out to sea with the returned message-in-a-bottle in her hand. Her map had been found and returned to her unused. She let it fall from her hands and watched it thud deep in the sand below.

A quiet puppy whine whimpered from behind and she turned to see the wolf laying down at her side, his nose nuzzling her hand for attention. She scratched his massive head and grinned in curious appreciation,

"Where did you come from?"

He creeped up on his belly closer to her and laid his great fury head in her lap looking up at her with careworn eyes. She bent down to kiss between his ears and he licked the tears off her cheek.

Suddenly crying out in pain and shock, Gentle stiffened. The wolf stood instantly on defense growling and looking around, confused as to what was happening. Gentle lifted her hand and slowly brought it across her body to the opposite shoulder. The wolf moved to see what she held. It was an arrow. There was a thick, spiked arrow sticking out of her upper arm, solid in its new hold. Gentle breathed ragged and slow in pain as she tried to rise to her feet. The wolf ducked under her and carried her on his back all the way to the Lighthouse and up into the Presence of the Physician at the top.

Pacing the hallway he waited until the Physician assured him she would be fine.

"There is no long term harm done, but she will need to rest. There will need to be much rest taken in the next weeks." Elohim looked at his man-wolf and asked, "Will you sit with her?"

The wolf rose up to his full height, shifting into his true bipedal form and swore,

"I will not leave her side."

When Gentle was at work that night, it was quiet and few customers needed her attention so she continued to calmly make her place one of order and efficiency. There was buoyancy in her step despite her recent broken heart and she smiled with the confidence of one with true friends and dear companions. She bustled about, mildly distracted, but still attending to cleaning and the half wall that hung down over the collection tubs continued where it always was as concrete walls are not inclined to move. It was in this very immovability that Gentle met with it as her head rose up from underneath quickly and sharply. The shock reverberated deep.

Her first reaction was to giggle in embarrassment. Everyone had hit their head on this same silly wall. In fact, this was the third time she had done it herself. But as she stood and the world about her spun, the throbbing began to nauseate and disorient her and she flung her hands out to the wall for solidity, moaning,

"Oh crap." She breathed slowly, "I just hit that *really* hard."

She felt so guilty. She always felt guilty when she put other people out. Her poor manager had been called in from home to take her to the emergency room. It was late at night and they sat silently in the waiting room as the hours continued. Gentle wanted to make conversation so as to apologize and ease the awkwardness of the situation, but all she could do was grip the wheel chair with both hands so her disorientation wouldn't see her fall out to the ground.

No work for a couple weeks as the tests confirmed nothing more than a concussion. But the doctor warned that such injuries dealt differently with each patient. The statistics say that 30% of concussion sufferers recovered in three months, 90% recovered within six months. Gentle couldn't help wonder what happened to the last 10%.

She rested at home feeling even worse as she watched Mercy take on all her duties on top of everything else with which she was already dealing. LaMa tottered around and Gentle nattered as best as she could with her from the couch. What happened when the care giver needed care given?

Gentle tried to not get too angry as she recalled how many times in the last twelve months she had requested that wall be made safer. How many times, all the other associates had hit their heads and how many times she had verbally made known her concern for a safer work space. None of it documented. None of it acted on. All of it ignored. She tried to shake her head in frustration, but stopped and clung to her skull in immediate discomfort.

Gentle sighed texting back to Manly trying not to sound too grumpy. He remained her constant companion sending her funny pictures and smiles all day long.

The Wolf took up his duties on the front porch constant, vigilant, and ever ready to defend those who could not stand alone.

A shallow river dreamed of in faerie tales.

Chapter 19

Mercy was slowly breathing easier. There was still much to be done, but the light at the end of the tunnel, that had been another train, passed in due time and now she saw another light beyond, only this time, there was a breath of fresh air accompanying it.

Mercy considered the mire of all her life in the past year and began to see stepping stones rise up. Yes, she just might get to the other side after all. She was grateful that Gentle stayed with her continually and they enjoyed each other's company alongside and alone together.

Gentle returned to work with injury restrictions fairly quickly for a speedy healing. She always considered herself to be a hypochondriac therefore she tried to push herself toward health with earnest guilt. But after only two weeks saw her return to regular duties, the weight of a simple box needing to be moved was enough to trigger some form of over exertion in her head again. Not wanting to be a bother, she simply had Mercy take her home early, but within forty-eight hours, Mercy almost had to carry her back into the emergency room and thus began four days of hospital stay over, followed by two and a half months of bed and couch ridden inactivity.

Much of this post concussive injury consisted of very little pain, but more a constant dizziness and discomfort medically proven to not be vertigo, but just a healing process taking a long time. Gentle commiserated within herself and tried to avoid depression by spending almost all of her time in meditation.

The sights, the wonders, and the victories of revelation that occurred within her spirit blew her mind even more than a concrete wall and heavy box ever could. And through it all, every day, every hour, her constant friend and companion through technology stayed with her. Manly made her smile, he listened to her vent. He connected with her despite the distance of geography and chronology and the two found something strongly akin to love.

Gentle confessed to Mercy,

"My being so much older than Manly is becoming less and less important the more I get to know him."

Mercy smiled rather sarcastically,

"You know he's me, right?"

Gentle looked confused so Mercy offered explanation,

"Quess was over twenty years older than I."

"Yeah, but he was perfect for you and you were in love," retorted Gentle too quickly. Mercy just raised her eyebrow and Gentle conceded.

Manly was eighteen years younger than she. She had never met him in person, but had known him for over three years now and this last year they had been constant friends, talking almost every day. She admitted casting him into the friend zone because he was too young, but recalled the last few men she had dated who were equal or older in age to her, and recognized that this Manly was more a man for her than any of these older gentlemen had proved to be. It was only her concern for his family's acceptance of her and dealing with all the teasing that would eventually surface that kept her back from seeking a more significant companionship with him. And since when did she ever not do something just because she was afraid? Since Never. So she decided to let herself learn to love him and hoped he could learn to love her also.

Mercy observed their friendship as it grew in significance and encouraged her sister,

"I do believe this is the healthiest relationship you have ever had with a male."

Gentle laughed and agreed,

"Who'd 'a thunk it, right?" She looked out the window and counted the three and then the four crows that landed in the back yard. "New partnerships and new beginnings" she mused, "I have no idea when we'll ever meet, or if we ever will? But for now, I am content to get to know him without the confusion of physical chemistry that has always muddled my thinking in the past."

Mercy teased,

"What a novel concept."

Gentle considered blushing but recalled that her meanderings along Guilt Road had often led her directly to the Kingdom of the Coyote Conglomeration. Instead, she decided that all her past life with its messes and mistakes was what had brought her to where she stood now and where she stood now was good ground and she liked it. No guilt or regret only contented peace and goodwill for the road ahead. Yes, she was embarrassed by past actions and sorry to have hurt those she loved, but looking ahead was the only way to repay the past with healing in her present and hope in her future. So Gentle just laughed at herself with Mercy. There really was no better thing to do, and hearing Mercy laugh again sounded so good.

She celebrated her joy found in pain with Immanuel on her island. They walked the peninsular together and explored the edges of her subconscious spirit in communion. She loved this time spent alone with Him, but she had a question that burned within as she saw the wolf observing her from the edge of the forest. She couldn't wait to join him but paused before running to his side and asked of her Comforter,

"I don't understand how he got here?" She looked up at the sky remembering what Wolfy had suggested in teasing, that he'd fallen from above.

Immanuel just smiled and asked her with a loving and implied "dah",

"Who do you think build that?" He nodded to the cabin then winked at her and pushed her toward her companion. She skipped off to play with her friend and giggled. So it wasn't really *her* island after all.

She clambered onto the back of the great Wolf and he took off running through the trees not stopping until they reached a serenely wooded glade. There was a cozy den hidden on the far side, but he brought her to the shallow river and returned to his bipedal form holding her hand and leading her along in a romance of gentle care that she had only ever dreamed of in fairy-tales.

Hobo's spirit returns faithfully to LaMa and Bumbles.

Chapter 20

The heat of summer would soon begin lazily melting into brisk falling winds and in this late season, Gentle discovered the last of the fruit trees in her orchard was a plum tree. He proudly displayed his one fruit just within reach. She plucked it with thanks and tested the sweetness. It might be a year or so yet for full appreciation. She sucked her cheeks in and flapped her tongue laughing in delight at the sour, but honorable produce so proudly born by a young tree.

The heavy mooing of the two added heifers in the cow field sounded belabored and Gentle kept a keen eye open for signs of new birth. The farmer who rented the field had told her it could be any day now and likely just in that one moment when she wasn't looking.

A hot wind with cold finger tips blustered up under her hair and the country girl looked to seek out any threatening green in the sky that might hint of a tornado. It was still a simple grey, but the clouds were loud with summer thunder. She called to the cats and assisted Hobo up the front steps and into LaMa's bedroom where he crashed on his sleeping pad. LaMa was scolding someone in her sleep, something about being kind and not mean.

"Hey hon," Gentle caressed the elderly arm to comfort her awake, "I have pills and juice for you this morning."

"Oh dear," LaMa croaked quietly out of slumber, "I was dreaming of my sister."

Gentle helped her sit up and handed her the tiny cup of medications. LaMa poured them into her mouth and continued chattering through her teeth,

"She was being mean so I was telling her to be nice."

"I heard" encouraged the companion, "it was quite a good sermon."

LaMa giggled and shifted about to keep talking when Gentle reminded her,

"Take a drink, hon. Swallow what's in your mouth."

"Oh, yes." LaMa complied then creakily lay back down again. "What time is it?"

"Time for a big storm, I think," Gentle looked out the window. "We're headed into some rainy days, so they say."

"Well, we need the rain." LaMa drifted off again.

Hobo gave a doggy huff, just as tired, and slipped away to slumber by her side.

Gentle stumbled back to the couch. These days her head only allowed her to be up for about an hour until she needed to return to horizontal immovability, but she was glad to be vertical if only for a small time in between long rests.

She texted Manly and they took another walk on the Island together, his mind and his imagination matching hers heartbeat for heartbeat. They stopped inside the comforts of the cabin a while and Gentle sighed in deep contentment looking forward to the day when their physical realms would align and they could sit as they did here; he working on his projects at the table, she on her artistry by the fire. He brought such soothing to her wild soul as she had never known before. This was a long awaited love.

The storms outside raged on, but inside there was community, laughter and much healing until the last day of the storm when LaMa stood in the doorway calling for her loyal Hobo.

Gentle stepped onto the porch peering through the rain and calling out into the wind,

"Hobo," but he was nowhere in sight.

"He came and woke me this morning when I was in bed," explained LaMa sitting on the couch with Bumbles who was grooming her fur and leaving puffs of it all over on the distracted lady's lap. "He put his face on the mattress and snuffed at me. I think he might have been saying goodbye." Her eyes watered a little, "I let him out then and I haven't seen him since."

Gentle relayed the story to Mercy that evening. She just sighed and admitted,

"His body is close to shutting down completely." She whispered what Gentle already knew, "He won't survive long out in this weather."

The all had an uneasy sleep that night as the winds and rain thrashed about the little house on the hill.

Gentle's phone rang as she fixed breakfast and pills for LaMa the next morning. It was Mercy,

"I think I found Hobo," she said and Gentle's dreaded hope tugged within her heart. "I think I saw him by the corner at the bottom of the ditch on my way out but I was already running late. I'm not sure though, so could you check?"

"No worries." Gentle assured her sister, but kept the news to herself as she helped LaMa settle at the breakfast table. She rested a moment to regain strength in her head and then went for a morning walk in the post rain-washed sunshine.

Pulling a wheeled cart slowly behind, Gentle made her way down the road to the corner where she noticed a hole in the ditch weeds. From the top of the roadside, Gentle followed what looked like a mud slide down the hill into the neighboring farmer's barbed fencing and there underneath was a wretched bundle of black and white, mud splattered fur. Gentle's heart sank as she prepared to carry the body back to the farm. But her heart sank even more as she got up close and saw the tiniest of ragged panting coming from the open gasping mouth.

She hailed down a passing pickup and the furry body, barely clinging to life, was carefully carted back to the house where Mercy returned quickly. The girls then drove to the closest emergency vet clinic.

Hobo had said his personal goodbye's to LaMa and now hung on with the last shred of loyal dogginess to give his final affection to the girls. And as he sighed his last peaceful breath, cared for and petted with deep love, he passed on. In the skies outside, he touched noses with the quiet Hawk, newly returned to these parts, and journeyed back to his companion to sit at her feet in spirit for as long as she needed him there.

Mercy told LaMa the sad news on their return and she nodded with tears in her eyes,

"He came and said goodbye to me this morning when I was in bed." There was no need to correct the timing.

The warmth of a den holds comfort and safety.

Chapter 21

The weeks following Hobo's passing were very difficult. There was no kindness in LaMa's random memory. She forgot how many times she repeated the same sentence. She forgot if she'd had her pills or even if she'd eaten any food. She forgot what day it was, unless it was Sunday when remarkably she knew every week it was time to go to mass. But sadly (and as it should be), she could never forget she had lost her dog.

"I need another dog" complained LaMa sitting with Bumbles on her lap and Meh sitting at her shoulder on the back of the couch. Master was curled up at the aloof end of the couch.

Gentle negotiated between mother and daughter. Mercy didn't think she could bear the burden of another dependent creature. She just sighed and rolled her eyes at Gentle and left to answer her phone in the privacy of her bedroom. Gentle encouraged her,

"We're keeping our eyes open."

"Well, I need another dog." Her eye's brightened at another thought. "We should get a pig too, and feed all the extra rotting cucumbers and tomatoes in the garden to him."

"And will you be the one to feed and care for this pig because I know I don't have time." Gentle smirked in mild frustration at the all too familiar carousel of conversation.

"I can," determined LaMa. "I need to get a ladder to trim those top branches off the tree out there too," she gazed out the front window. "Those branches are dead and they need to come off."

"I'm not sure that the idea of you on a ladder is all that good?" remarked her companion.

"Oh, I don't care." LaMa discarded the concern. "I'm fine. I don't care if I die. All my family has died except my brother."

Gentle set the dinner plates on the table and let Mercy know servings were ready as LaMa continued,

"My father told me I would be late for my own funeral. But I'm ready to go if I need to."

"Well, I'm not ready for you to be gone yet." Gentle firmly handed her the evening dosages and sat to enjoy the meal.

"Well, you're too sweet." The elderly lady lowered her voice a little, "you be sure to stay here with Mercy when I'm gone and look after her."

Gentle ginned at the conspiracy of the stern mother who rarely showed her affections overtly,

"I believe Mercy looks after me, more than I look after her."

"Oh, you're a good girl." She patted her hand then continued the merry-go-round, "I need another dog."

Mercy sat to join them ignoring the spinning conversation,

"That was Quess' daughter. She's coming to get Macro tomorrow."

Gentle was sad to think her new equestrian compadre would leave so soon.

"What time," was all she said?

"After lunch." Mercy noshed on the dinner enjoying the simplicity of food.

"K, then." Gentle ate also.

"Mercy, you need to get me another dog," ordered her mother.

A hush fell on the table as a lonely howl sang to the stars outside.

Gentle finished quickly, neatly stacked the plates by the sink then slipped out the mud porch door, headed toward the gully.

When she was out of sight of the house, she shivered into her greater feline form and slunk through the scrubland.

The dark night held no alarm for her and she was much comforted by the deep quiet, until the shadows started moving. It was not the movement that concerned the lioness for she was agile and strong. It was what she recognized moving in the shadows and the large number of them that was cause for great concern.

Prince Don led the attack. There was no time to set up defenses. The ambush was well ordered and too quickly Gentle was cornered, surrounded and encroached upon all sides. They attacked without hesitation and the lioness form fought back swiftly and with great strength casting coyote after coyote off her back but she could not hold them off for long. Their intensity was just too great. Scrambling beneath the teeth and claws, Gentle was dazed and confused by the attack set upon her and fell out of form in quivering agony as a frightened heap of a woman, fragile and dependent.

Suddenly there was a swift rush and Prince Don let out a sharp bark of pain. Confusion swirled as fur and claws ferociously flew about the poor girl and she cowered on the ground in tears.

A massive snarl in her ear snapped her to attention as she felt great jaws closing around her neck. She was being dragged unceremoniously off into the darkness. Striking out she slammed her fists into the face that held her. It growled back loudly, the fear reverberated all down her spine. She was tossed against a black wall, but before she could pull her senses together a barking growl forced her to the ground again. Then it was gone and the sounds of a terrible battle scraped at the scrublands just outside this newer warm darkness that held her close.

A small whine at her elbow startled her and the little red fox nudged in to calm her shivering. She picked up the little fellow and held him tight breathing slowly. The battle outside continued and Gentle's curiosity pushed against her shock. Still carrying the little red comfort, the trembling woman tiptoed toward the opening and was horrified to see half of the coyotes who'd attacked her lying disemboweled around the opening of the cave while the other half continued attacking the great dire wolf holding his ground in the fray.

Prince Don was slowly coming too, but with his throat was lacerated so deeply he could barely speak to round up his crew. He tried a howl that bubbled out of his spewing red throat just loud enough to draw their attention and they all turned tail in an instant and disappeared with him.

The wolf suddenly turned on her and snarled in his bloody frenzy. She stood her ground though, frozen in both shock and wonder.

The little red fox jumped from her arms and began sniffing and picking through the pockets of the dead coyotes muttering about finders keepers.

The wolf shook his head and sneezed.

"Are you hurt," Gentle inquired?

He shrugged,

"They weren't after me." He trotted up toward her slowly.

"Thank you," was all the shy girl could muster to whisper.

He nudged her with his head back toward his den. She followed with her hand buried deep into his fur. The little red fox watched them enter and took up his own sentry position on the top of the cave entrance howling his friend's victory to the sky making sure all nearby knew that this was *his* friend.

Wolfy circled the mossy bed a few times then curled up and tilted his head expectantly waiting for her to join him. She stepped in between his great paws and leaned against his belly snuggling against the warm softness.

"I'm guessing we may not hear from the Conglomeration for a while, now," she said closing her eyes in comfort and security.

"Likely not," was all the wolf said as he curled around the woman in his embrace and rested his head upon her lap.

She mumbled in sleepy peace,

"Don't ever leave me, Wolfy."

"I haven't yet and I have no plans to." He whispered then instantly fell sound asleep.

The Entrance to the dungeon amphitheater was secure.

Chapter 22

He knocked politely and cleared his throat discretely standing at the cave entrance. Gentle heard him and froze in her waking. Wolfy was still dead asleep.

"If you don't mind, or even if you do, quite frankly," he stepped in to fill the doorway, "you will be accompanying me to my dungeons now."

The Coyote King snapped his fingers and thick black chains clamped themselves around the sleeping wolf who was suddenly, painfully aware of the horrible conscious reality. He growled and tried snapping and breaking free only to find the chains pull closer in on him. In fact the more he struggled the tighter his bonds became. Gentle laid a silent hand on his fur to calm him. This was all too familiar to her.

They were dragged over the fields in the early morning pitch dark, Wolfy fighting against the chains that only harmed more the more he fought. Gentle walked quietly beside him. She saw him hesitate in his wrestling only long enough to lick an old wound that she hadn't noticed before. In the very crook of his front leg, right next to his heart, there was a black pad of scarred skin, thick, rough and barely exposed underneath his fluffy carriage. Each time the chains pressed in against him, the skin seemed to bulge like a pocket of puss. At one time, Gentle thought she saw odd movement beneath. She kept a closer eye on it as a new understanding began formulating in her heart.

The Conglomeration caravan took its prisoners underneath the great black regal glade of the Coyote King to the central dungeons where they were deposited together in a gladiatorial ring. Wolfy was on high alert. He whispered to Gentle,

"Get behind me. I can take whatever they bring out to fight us."

Gentle's heart sank.

The King laughed as Wolfy's whisper carried with perfect acoustic clarity in the amphitheater.

"Your geometric understanding fails you in your delusion, I'm afraid, Sir Wolf." King Coyote scoffed. "What part of two bodies in the center of a circle has any protection from without? Hmmm?" He looked at Gentle knowing she understood the answer.

Clanking chains pulled up various doors around the central dirt floor and a thousand tiny swords were shoved in toward the two. A thousand tiny brown gladiators hesitated in their task, more terrified of the snapping, barking and laughing coming from the coyote spectators than they were at the prospect of attacking a girl and the dire wolf capable of devouring all their tiny little selves in just a few bites . . . except that he was in chains.

The noble wolf snapped to attention spinning and pacing under the weight of the crunching and pressing chains. He circled his lady, keeping his tail at her heart.

"Don't turn your back on me, Wolfy." Gentle called to him above the chanting of the crowd.

Wolfy growled,

"Stay behind me! I've got this."

"Wolfy, stop!" Gentle called to him again, but he ignored her, snarling at the circling crowd of Brownie Gladiators.

Gentle looked into the shadows of dust and saw with eyes learned in the ways of darkness. She saw them, the snapping teeth and grinding paws of Coyote Sentries pressing the Brownies in toward them. The littlest ones in the back were coerced forward and whipped if they hesitated. She screamed at her defender again,

"Wolfy, stop!"

The wolf continued with his back to her, circling her, protecting her, preparing to pounce even against the cutting weight of his own chains.

The Coyote King gargled in his laughter drunk on the excess of agony.

Gentle grappled with the chains around Wolfy's face, pulling with superhuman strength to turn him around. He snapped at her, infuriated that she should hinder him in such a way, but she fought back until, against his will, he stared her ruthlessly in the face.

"What are you doing!" He screamed at her.

"Do not turn your back on me." Gentle stared him down.

"I have to." His eyes shifted across the horde of tiny gladiators. They were close enough to attack now. "I have to protect you."

His body was almost doubled up on himself as the chains cinched tighter. She saw the agony and fury dissolving his sense of reason.

"They are not the enemy here." Gentle forced him to attend to her.

Wolfy started with a sudden yip. The tiny spears, barely piercing his outer skin, were already pricking at him like dutiful pins forced into a packed pin cushion. He squirmed and tried to move, but the restraints were cutting through and the bleeding burned against the chafing. He looked confused, dazed and completely misunderstood her attentions.

"Wolfy." Her voice was calm and sang softly through the chaos. "Wolfy, darling, I need my man."

"What do you think I'm trying to do?" He accused her in rising fury.

"You can't even move, right now." She ran her fingers down his long nose with tears from her eyes splashing on his face.

"I have to be strong. I have to protect you." He strained with all his might and the chains constricted, rending fur from raw flesh. The Wolf screamed in defiance.

Gentle roared and instantly became the great lioness, terrifying the thousand Brownies with her sudden expanse. They rioted against the guards behind them, pushed back with their own fright and disappeared into the depths of the dungeons again leaving a suffocating dust cloud in their wake.

Wolfy coughed and peered through the settling cloud. Gentle stood before him again in womanly form, strong, settled and calm.

"You saved me, my darling." She kissed his nose, "please, let me save you back."

There in the center of the ring of dust, crushed and beaten on the floor, Wolfy collapsed.

He just looked up at her with pain throbbing in his eyes.

Gentle smiled and repeated,

"I need my man."

He had nothing left as the beast. If they were to die tonight, then at least they could die together. He shifted. Shivering into his naked bipedal form, He stood before his lady, ashamed of his weakness, vulnerable and utterly exposed.

She reached out to him and he embraced her, holding her close.

"I'm sorry I'm not strong enough to protect you." He apologized defeated.

She giggled.

He thought she could be insane.

She giggled again.

Stepping back he just stared at her, but she wasn't looking at him, she nodded at the ground behind him.

Manly turned to look through the clearing dust and saw a massive pile of chains, chains too big for a human to lift, or to be constrained by. He stood small before them, freed from their oppression. He was dumbfounded.

But a slow and steady, bored applause broke into his confusion.

"I'd say I was impressed, but I'd be lying, so . . . I'm impressed." The Coyote King winked at Gentle. Then he smirked and leaned back comfortably on his massive couch and sighed, gesturing to his brother lying limply on a couch next to him barely able to move due to his injuries. "You're going to want to be awake for this one, brother."

Prince Don Coyote tried to sit up as best as he could and watched the couple alone and silent in the center of the amphitheater dome.

Alf was a revoltingly adorable little schnauzer.

Chapter 23

The lights in the dome blacked out except for one tiny spot light that shone upon the ornate table torture lamp that had once held Meh, but now held the glowing red of their little fox friend.

"I'm sorry," was all he whimpered.

Without a second thought Manly pounced at the table again taking form as the wolf, and although he was still injured, his weight was enough to break the bonds and the fox fell free. But instead of making his escape, the little red fox drew his own dagger and plunged it deep into the half hidden black pad of skin under Wolfy's leg. The Wolf stopped shocked by the attack. It was as if a switch inside him had flipped and he crumbled to the ground.

The red fox backed away, dropping the dagger with horror filled eyes. He desperately apologized to Gentle, backing further and further away and then turned tail and ran down into the deepest parts of the dungeons. Gentle approached cautiously. There was a hush in the air as everyone watched what would happen next.

The gash in the old scar seeped putrid black ooze and from inside little withered limbs began tearing out and creating an even bigger wound. Snickering could be heard and a tiny imp clambered up from the open stench. He scrambled to the surface and crawled up to the very face of the shocked canine, mocked him and then disappeared off into the stadium seating like a great warrior claiming a victory lap. The crowd screamed wildly in delight.

Gentle rushed to Wolfy's side and lifted his head to her lap. She looked accusingly at the Coyote King who was watching so intently, she realized, his game was not yet up. She looked down and saw the puppy instincts kick in as Wolfy licked at the sore place to sooth his pain.

"No!" Gentle tried to pull his jaw away in time, but too late. His tongue lapped at the scar and the black ooze slid quickly, hungrily down his throat.

Wolfy shuddered. His eyes flickered at her in apologetic horror before being drowned in a pool of black from within.

Gentle backed up quickly and Wolfy stood slowly stretching his muscles as the black seeped through all his body and sealed over his wounds like tar. He took one look at her and growled a long, quiet resentful howl. Gentle shifted into lioness dreading what was about to happen.

She barely held him off as their battle raged; he with darkened intent to harm, she with intent to do as little harm as possible, yet she was not without her own raging weakness. It was not long until both surrendered to the fury within and claw for claw, tooth for tooth, and blood for blood was exchanged.

They fought on and on. It was impossible to see into the amphitheater and the crowd began dispersing either bored or busy with their own mischief. Even the King got bored and left with a yawn.

The size and intensity of the two crashed them through the walls and chained gates of the dungeons. But the state of the place they were in was such that fights were commonplace and the crowd simply adjusted their own self-absorbed contentions to make room for the two as they rumbled through the hallways and made their way in ferocious aggression to the surface.

They flickered in and out of dimensions. The Island was not immune to their snarling for they were intent upon expending the rage that fueled their fury. Slowing in spurts they circled each other, both apologetic, but unable to stop, their attacks too great to allow for simple forgiveness. They couldn't stop the fight now for they knew each had gone too far and when the dust would settle, the distance between them would be too torn, too ragged, and too far apart.

But as with all storms, they blew themselves out. Gentle sat on the paddock hilltop, dripping in sweat and blood, Manly sat beside her in a similar state. They touched hands briefly for a moment then parted, each looking back in sorrow filled glances.

Gentle turned to walk across the parking lot to the house. She wandered past Quess's daughter in the driveway. She was tugging and pulling, coercing and begging Macro to get into the trailer. Macro looked out of the corner of his fighting equestrian eyes. He saw Gentle and called to her silently,

"Don't make me leave," he begged.

Gentle looked away. She had no rights with the horse. He belonged to someone else. She could never keep him. She knew his well-being would likely be better here on Springhill Farm, but there was nothing she could do. She had to let him go. She plodded up to the house, and down to her bedroom. The Lighthouse was now her only refuge.

At dinner that night, Mercy shared the excellent news of an offer she'd received to buy the old family farm house at a price just enough to cover the land of Springhill Farm. The small acreage upon which the house on the hill sat was all that would be left on her mortgage. This was much relief to Mercy and it showed in her peace.

Gentle relayed the basic details of her fight with Manly.

Mercy encouraged her by pointing out that such toxic wounds were not the kind Gentle had any control over. Both girls had seen the extreme end of such things in the death of Quess. Gentle prayed that healing would be sought quickly. It was up to Manly now, only the Physician of Love could give any true healing.

LaMa reminded them that they needed another dog.

"How is the herd taking the loss of Macro?" Gentle inquired of her sister.

"Zoe is being broody and bossing the other two around. Poor old Codger is just cranky and Shyner is 'dupe-de-doing' along as always," Mercy snickered. "I'd like to try and get another horse to even the numbers out. They like it better when there's an even number."

"When will you get another horse?" LaMa asked.

"I don't know," Mercy replied distractedly looking at her phone and scrolling through something that suddenly caught her attention.

"Oh, crap," She sighed with resignation and showed Gentle the picture and family update that came to her from a cousin.

Gentle read the brief message under a picture of the most revoltingly adorable little black schnauzer pup:

"Alf needs a new home as he doesn't get along with the new baby."

Gentle raised her eyebrows as Mercy rolled her eyes back at her and shook her head.

"I give up, fine." Mercy went off to her room to call her cousin out of LaMa's hearing.

Take a turn around a new corner into the setting sun.

Chapter 24

Gentle's sons were joining her for the weekend again and she and Mercy had plans for them to help rake and burn leaves, and enjoy other bonfire shenanigans. But, Gentle had some serious business to be done first.

She descended to her chambers again with deep sorrow. It seemed the storms of her life kept blowing all interested gentlemen away and the battle with depression encroached upon her broken heart. She wanted to believe Manly would not forsake her entirely, but in this twilight hour, reason and reality were setting with the sun. The darkness must be faced. The Light was her only refuge.

Gentle petitioned the Throne of Grace and received all favor upon her for the sake of His glory. She took with her all she needed and stepped out from there with all authority available to her in Heaven and on Earth bound up in a small scroll of paper.

Her walk across the back fields was cold and the Kingdom of the Conglomeration loomed large. Yet, Gentle was steadfast in her determination and at peace in Who was by her side. As she entered the black gates she was generally ignored all around. It seemed her last fight here had made her much less of a threat and more as one who held rights of citizenship. She wasn't sure that was such a good thing.

The king ignored her until she stood before him in his banqueting hall where all the dark ones gorged themselves upon the pain and suffering of any who became a victim to their mischief.

"Yes?" He inquired with a mouthful of fresh meat, feigning boredom as always.

Gentle stepped up and handed the scroll to the king,

"I'm serving you your eviction notice."

He stopped his royal chewing with bloody saliva dribbling on his chin and a hush came over the hall.

"What?" He mocked. He would have disregarded her entirely but for the seal on the scroll.

"I'm evicting you." Gentle stood calmly. "You no longer have rights to squat anywhere within my atmosphere."

The King just stared at the scroll. Prince Don, recovered enough to gorge at the table also, snatched it up and tore it open. He read,

NOTIFICATION OF EVICTION

This certifies that the Coyote Conglomeration and its King, the Regent and Prince of this Present Darkness, and all who dwell to

follow and serve him with malicious intent are hereby upon receipt of this notice evicted from the presence and atmosphere of the one who carries and delivers this notification.

The reason for this eviction notice is:

-The continued efforts by this Present Darkness to obstruct, manipulate, and make unclear any and all parts of the rightful relationship of the bearer of this notification with The Creator, Elohim.

-All debts and payments owed to this Present Darkness by the holder of this title of eviction have been paid once for all by the Champion Defender and Advocate, Immanuel.

-Any further arguments or accusations against the bearer of this notice, by the Regent of this Present Darkness must be made in person before the Throne of Grace.

This decree is handed down with all Authority given by the Name JESUS and is indisputable now and forevermore. Amen.

Prince Don hushed and stared back and forth between the claimant and the served.

The King set down his meat and wiped his face. Settling back into his chair he looked at Gentle squarely, and inquired,

"This sounds important. But how do you propose to back up this claim?"

"I don't need to." She spoke an incantation,

"The Presence of the Living GOD is in this place."

A wind began blowing through the halls and Gentles wings began billowing out behind her. The butterfly wings stretched out and the dusted mist of Love began to swirl as a cloud about her. The top wings stretched as far up and out as they could until the thick black veins that outlined the brilliant colors of light suddenly cracked and shattered, falling off her like chains in the darkness, still shuddering, the wings fluffed into feathers of every shade and blend, color and hue of the rainbow seen only by the citizens of Heaven. Gentle continued her chanting,

"Holy is His people who glory in His Grace."

The second set of wings, unfurled in all their blinding brilliance of Faith unseen, unheard, and unstoppable. A sudden wave of light burst out from the center of these pure white wings and in its wake every being of darkness was pushed back in a blast that left them scattered, and flattened to the ground. Only the Dark Regent remained in place, yet the emanating pulse accompanied with the ever sweeping mist of Love crumbled him just enough to force him to fall with knee cracking injury to his humility.

Gentle continued softly whispering with such acoustic deafening that all within the dark clamped their hands tight over their ears to shut it out,

"Hallelujah and Amen, forever on bended knee"

Then she too fell to her knees with a cry of pain as the base wings, the sharp dragon scales of speed where ripped out from her back by the root and a new set, larger, faster, and heavier with feathers of deep green and high blues were implanted by unseen hands. The surgery was swift, complete and the healing set to take hold. Gentle's body shuddered in agonizing relief and she lifted herself up from where her hands had caught her fall and knelt upward with all the height that complete humbled surrender can offer. She cried aloud,

"Glory for Thy Kingdom comes; draw near to me."

The ground beneath burst up about them as geysers of dust and muck and the entire ground level of the Conglomeration with gates and halls, chambers and quarters disintegrated into multiple dimensions round about them. All that was left kneeling was the Regent, alone in his darkness.

"This is not over," he glared at her, eye to eye, in forced obeisance. "I will never stop pursuing you."

Gentle slowly waved her new wings and stood to her feet,

"And I will never stop resisting you with Love." The mist swirling about her wafted around in the darkness. The Regent's outer being began slowly dissolving in the mist, as metal to acid, but yet he resisted.

From the shadows of the depths beneath crept a thousand and more tiny soldiers, freed from their servitude with the dissolution of the Conglomeration. The dungeons, the stolen national halls of Brownie pride, long since taken over by the Coyotes, were now restored and the tiny fae sought out their completed victory.

Gentle welcomed them into the Light and continued her pronouncement to that thief,

"And, I will never stop telling them, everyone who cares to hear, that Elohim loves them."

And the Prince of this Present Darkness fled.

NOTIFICATION OF EVICTION

This certifies that the

Coyote Conglomeration and its King,

the Regent and Prince of this Present Darkness,

and all who dwell to follow and serve him with malicious intent

are hereby upon receipt of this notice evicted from the presence and atmosphere of the

one who carries and delivers this notification.

The reason for this eviction notice is:

-The continued efforts by this Present Darkness to obstruct, manipulate, and make unclear any and all parts of the rightful relationship of the bearer of this notification with

The Creator, Elohim.

-All debts and payments owed to this Present Darkness by the holder of this title of eviction have been paid once for all by the

Champion Defender and Advocate, Immanuel.

-Any further arguments or accusations against the bearer of this notice, by the Regent of this Present Darkness must be made in person before the Throne of Grace.

This decree is handed down with all Authority given by the Name JESUS and is indisputable now and forevermore. Amen.

New growth is restored to the Brownie Nation.

Chapter 25

Gentle heard a small whine coming from behind some rubble and noticed a little red nose, also having crept up out of the depths, sniffing the air about him in fear.

"It's ok." She encouraged the red fox, "it's safe to come out now."

He slunk toward her, tail between his legs, in utter disgrace. She knelt down, her new wings still tender, but flowing freely behind her. She reached out to let him sniff the dusty mist that still glowed about her person. He approached tentatively afraid that he too might dissolve as the Coyote King had begun to.

"It's quite safe, if you aren't allergic to Love."

He sniffed and his eyes widened in delight, sniffing more, then stepping in closer he breathed as deeply as he could relaxing in the peace of unconditional love. Somewhat recovered, he apologized,

"I'm so sorry... I ..."

Gentle hushed him,

"Shh, that is not for me to be concerned with. The past is done and the present is where we are now. I believe all things will work for the best future."

The little fox blushed.

"Besides," she acknowledged, "It needed to be done." She looked out the corner of her eye with a wry smile and added, "I could have been done *better* but you did as you did as well as you could, so that is enough of that." She kissed his little nose, "Besides, you have a bigger need to focus on right now."

The Brownies twittered in the near distance and followed the example of the fox, closing in cautiously upon the dust cloud and breathing in the fresh scent of acceptance, each little fae creature finding refreshing healing within the swirling, dusty light.

"Like what?" The fox was completely confused.

Gentle smiled at him. She encouraged,

"This nation," she gestured to the Brownies, "have been victims of slavery for some generations now. They will need someone to show them how to live freely."

The fox scoffed,

"I can't take care of an entire creature group?"

Gentle watched as the crowds inched closer in toward the fluffy red canine.

"They're already following your example."

He darted about in a circle around himself, chattering panicked,

"I know what you're getting at! I'm no king. It's a fun idea to tell stories about, but I can't be a king."

"Says who?" Gentle asked.

"Says me!" exclaimed the fox.

"So stop saying that." Gentle emphatically made her flittering way through the rubble upon her wings. With each rustle of the lowest pair, the green and blue feathers, she darted instantly here, and dashed immediately there, all over the glade. The upper rainbow feathers dusted their faery glow about and new growth began seeping over the destruction.

The red fox tried to keep up arguing with her the whole time. The Brownies couldn't help following him, chasing his big fluffy tail as if to play their first game of tag in all their childhood years. Their giggling grew louder with each round. This only annoyed the red fox and made him dash faster away from them, that in turn saw the little mischievous Brownies only chase him down all the more with such merriment as to make the scowliest of curmudgeons crack a grin.

Gentle laughed out loud and lead the merry parade across the fields toward the ravine and paddock hilltop. The red fox was kept busy with all the chasing and fussed at his followers with yips and barks, but they continued their play, just too delighted to be free to do as they wished.

By the time they reached the paddock where Gentle was greeted by the trio of equestrians on the hilltop, the red fox sat himself firmly on his buttocks and defiantly yelled,

"What am I supposed to do with this lot?"

The Brownies began weaving twigs and flowers into his fur. He scratched at their handiwork grumpily.

Gentle waved and blew him a kiss with parting instructions,

"Be kind, listen to their cares, and laugh. Laugh a lot!"

The fox plopped into a prostrate pose of frustrated resignation. The Brownies danced around him tossing flower petals, rusty leaves, and their own little magical laughter tinkled across the hilltop.

Mercy was in the coral throwing hay to a new painted horse. Gentle greeted them both,

"Hallo sister and welcome new friend."

"It never ceases to amaze me" said Mercy, "how some things can take a year and others, just a phone call." She patted the newest member of the Springhill herd on his nose. "His name is Magic." She continued. "I thought that quite appropriate."

Gentle smiled and agreed,

"Appropriate and fantastic," She walked toward the house, "I'll be fetching the boys a bit later. Did you want to do the bonfire tonight?"

Mercy nodded,

"The weather should be fine enough for even mom to come and sit with us. Also," Mercy continued, "Magic isn't the only new friend I brought home today."

"Alf is here?" Gentle looked up at the house.

"Not only is he here," Mercy snuffed in happy disgust, "He's already settled and established as a lap dog being fed cookies from mom's hand."

Gentle sighed,

"So much for giving him a healthy diet," But then she giggled knowing how happy it would make LaMa to spoil another dog.

A double portion of blessing arrived.

Chapter 26

As Gentle walked around to the back side of the house her heart lurched in pain at the sight of the hill in her back yard above the gully. Things with Manly were left so unsettled. They had maintained a cooling off period and Gentle hoped with all her heart that her young love could find his way to where he wanted to go, or at least maybe figure out where he wanted to go from here.

She slowly walked up toward the scrub in search of him. He was waiting for her, sitting outside the den as Wolfy, resting and recovering slowly from his deep wounds. She sat next to him.

"I'm sorry." He said, shifting into human form, sending his typical barking text,

"As am I," She responded.

"It's just . . . so much," He faltered.

"Yeah, yeah it is," she texted him in real time. For though he was very much with her in spirit, and their connection was strong, he was still physically living near to the other side of the country. Through all this, they still had never met. Gentle had to remind herself of that reality.

"Manly," she hesitated, "you have led me to believe you wished to pursue more of life together with me, but you have kept so much of your private heart hidden. Don't cheat me from the best parts of you, please?"

"I know." He was genuinely heartbroken.

"What do you want?" She asked.

"I am not prepared, at this time, to commit to anything long term." She could hear the pain tearing at his heart.

"I agree, and I'm not really asking for that. I only hope to continue pursuing a closer understanding of each other." She shrugged with mild amusement. "If I had the chance to step away from my life, I probably would too."

Glancing across the landscape of her crazy world she added, "My life is very messy. I am not an easy person to be with, but, I like my life." She smiled proudly to herself, "I love my messy life."

There was silence for a moment as Manly felt the crushing loneliness creep in and Gentle gathered up all the patience she could muster.

"I would like," Gentle encouraged, "to make room in my messy life for your messy life, someday in the future. That is, if you should like to live in a beautiful mess?"

"As you wish" was all he could answer.

"I have to get my sons now. We're having a family bonfire tonight." She wandered toward her car.

"I don't want you out of my picture," Manly called after her.

"So don't let me be." Gentle signed off, got in her car and drove off to get her sons with the radio turned up loud.

That night, around the bonfire, LaMa sat with a glass of wine offering tid-bits of her hotdog to Bumbles who continued to beg for food on her lap.

The disgustingly, adorable Alf dashed back and forth barking happily between the attentions of his new family and the boys. Manson and Sirreh chased him, throwing sticks for the pup to chase, and munched on s'mores and their own hotdogs.

Peaz leaned heavily upon Gentle, telling her tales of his latest mix-up fan fiction that starred himself, his stuffed toys, and various movie and television characters.

Master and Meh sat on top of the car in the parking lot above them quite disgusted at the prospect of having to dominate yet another pointless canine. Their twin heads moved in sync as they both kept a close eye on Alf's antics.

The horse herd, with Zoe still leading as a brood mare, gallivanted about as the newest member was adjusted in. Shyner was uncharacteristically motivated now that he had someone to boss around. Codger continued grumpy, and Magic lazily plodded back to eating each time someone tried to push him away.

Mercy leaned comfortably against a log, smoking the last of Quess' cigars, and sipping the last of his whiskey. She was lost in her own memories of grief and relief, content to be just where she was. This was her farm. This was her home. This was good after all. She smiled and then laughed out loud watching the cats try to subdue the effervescent delight of the new dog.

The old man hawk watched silently from one of the dead trees in the ravine, fluffing his contented feathers and beneath him, another celebration was underway. The Red Fox welcomed the Brownies into his life and they, in return, made all sorts of cheeky plans to frustrate and delight him.

Sirreh suddenly stopped chasing the dog around and counted the flock of crows that landed in the tree over the coral,

" . . . twelve!" He exclaimed excited, "for future prosperity and blessings."

"I can drink to that," cheered Gentle as she passed out sodas to her sons.

She looked around from her happy circle of family then gazed up to the hill to where a pair of yellow canine eyes blinked slowly at her.

She smiled at Wolfy as he limped along the top of the gully in full view. He then turned to follow his Alpha, the Great Physician, back to a place where healing might restore what once had infected him against his will.

He glanced back again toward her and called in his spirit,

"I'll be back."

She giggled a geeky giggle and responded,

"I know."

And thus, this story finds it's ending in the continuing of freedom in Faith, Hope, and Love. But the greatest of these is LOVE.

GLOSSARY

FAVORED AUTHORS

J.M. Barry (9 May 1860 – 19 June 1937)

-Peter Pan (and his all tales)

Douglas Adams (11 March 1952 – 11 May 2001)

-<u>The Hitchhiker's Guide to the Galaxy</u> series

May Gibbs (17 January 1877 – 27 November 1969

-<u>The Complete Adventures of Snugglepot and Cuddlepie</u>

Enid Blyton (11 August 1897 – 28 November 1968)

-just yes, almost all her children's novels and series'

C.S. Lewis (29 November 1898 – 22 November 1963)

-The Narnia Series

-<u>The Screwtape Letters</u>

J.R.R Tolkien (3 January 1892 – 2 September 1973)

-<u>The Hobbit</u>

-<u>Lord of the Rings</u>

FEATURED POETRY

Counting Crows Nursery Rhyme:

<u>Crows: An Old Rhyme</u> by Heidi Holder

One is for bad news

Two is for mirth

Three is a wedding

Four is a birth

Five is for riches

Six is a thief

Seven is a journey

Eight is for grief

Nine is a secret

Ten is for sorrow

Eleven is for love

Twelve is joy for tomorrow

My Country

By Dorothea Mackellar (1885 – 1968)

The love of field and coppice,
Of green and shaded lanes.
Of ordered woods and gardens
Is running in your veins,
Strong love of grey-blue distance
Brown streams and soft dim skies
I know but cannot share it,
My love is otherwise.

I love a sunburnt country,
A land of sweeping plains,
Of ragged mountain ranges,
Of droughts and flooding rains.
I love her far horizons,
I love her jewel-sea,
Her beauty and her terror -
The wide brown land for me!

A stark white ring-barked forest

All tragic to the moon,
The sapphire-misted mountains,
The hot gold hush of noon.
Green tangle of the brushes,
Where lithe lianas coil,
And orchids deck the tree-tops
And ferns the warm dark soil.

Core of my heart, my country!
Her pitiless blue sky,
When sick at heart, around us,
We see the cattle die-
But then the grey clouds gather,
And we can bless again
The drumming of an army,
The steady, soaking rain.

Core of my heart, my country!
Land of the Rainbow Gold,
For flood and fire and famine,
She pays us back threefold-
Over the thirsty paddocks,

Watch, after many days,

The filmy veil of greenness

That thickens as we gaze.

An opal-hearted country,

A wilful, lavish land-

All you who have not loved her,

You will not understand-

Though earth holds many splendours,

Wherever I may die,

I know to what brown country

My homing thoughts will fly.

Invictus

By William Ernest Henley

Out of the night that covers me,

Black as the Pit from pole to pole,

I thank whatever gods may be

For my unconquerable soul.

In the fell clutch of circumstance

I have not winced nor cried aloud.

Under the bludgeonings of chance

My head is bloody, but unbowed.

Beyond this place of wrath and tears

Looms but the Horror of the shade,

And yet the menace of the years

Finds, and shall find, me unafraid.

It matters not how strait the gate,

How charged with punishments the scroll.

I am the master of my fate:

I am the captain of my soul.

Saint Patrick's Breastplate Prayer

I arise today

Through a mighty strength, the invocation of the Trinity,

Through belief in the Threeness,

Through confession of the Oneness

of the Creator of creation.

I arise today

Through the strength of Christ's birth with His baptism,

Through the strength of His crucifixion with His burial,

Through the strength of His resurrection with His ascension,

Through the strength of His descent for the judgment of doom.

I arise today

Through the strength of the love of cherubim,

In the obedience of angels,

In the service of archangels,

In the hope of resurrection to meet with reward,

In the prayers of patriarchs,

In the predictions of prophets,

In the preaching of apostles,

In the faith of confessors,

In the innocence of holy virgins,

In the deeds of righteous men.

I arise today, through

The strength of heaven,

The light of the sun,

The radiance of the moon,

The splendor of fire,

The speed of lightning,

The swiftness of wind,

The depth of the sea,

The stability of the earth,

The firmness of rock.

I arise today, through

God's strength to pilot me,

God's might to uphold me,

God's wisdom to guide me,

God's eye to look before me,

God's ear to hear me,

God's word to speak for me,

God's hand to guard me,

God's shield to protect me,

God's host to save me

From snares of devils,

From temptation of vices,

From everyone who shall wish me ill,

afar and near.

I summon today

All these powers between me and those evils,

Against every cruel and merciless power

That may oppose my body and soul,

Against incantations of false prophets,

Against black laws of pagandom,

Against false laws of heretics,

Against craft of idolatry,

Against spells of witches and smiths and wizards,

Against every knowledge that corrupts man's body and soul;

Christ to shield me today

Against poison, against burning,

Against drowning, against wounding,

So that there may come to me an abundance of reward.

Christ with me,

Christ before me,

Christ behind me,

Christ in me,

Christ beneath me,

Christ above me,

Christ on my right,

Christ on my left,

Christ when I lie down,

Christ when I sit down,

Christ when I arise,

Christ in the heart of every man who thinks of me,

Christ in the mouth of everyone who speaks of me,

Christ in every eye that sees me,

Christ in every ear that hears me.

FEATURED SONGS

"Barbie Girl" by Aqua

"Bed of Roses" by Bon Jovi

"What does the Fox Say? By Ylvis

Photography Locations

(All photographs taken by Gregga J. Johnn)

Chapter 1	Springhill Farm, Iowa
Chapter 2	Private Chambers, Springhill Farm, Iowa
Chapter 3	Springhill Farm, Iowa
Chapter 4	Springhill Farm, Iowa
Chapter 5	The Barn at Springhill Farm, Iowa
Chapter 6	The hay field of Springhill Farm, Iowa
Chapter 7	"Nulla Point" at Cronulla Beach South, Australia
Chapter 8	The ravine (or glorified ditch), Springhill Farm, Iowa
Chapter 9	The garage and house, Springhill Farm, Iowa
Chapter 10	Basement apartment, Springhill Farm, Iowa
Chapter 11	The Esplanade, Cronulla Beach, Australia
Chapter 12	A random car sales lot in Marion, Iowa
Chapter 13	Wanda Beach parking lot, Australia
Chapter 14	Beneath the pear tree, Springhill Farm, Iowa
Chapter 15	Basement Apartment of Springhill Farm, Iowa
Chapter 16	The Coral and paddock hill with fields, Springhill Farm, Iowa
Chapter 17	Cronulla Beach south, Australia

Chapter 18	Paddock flowers, Springhill Farm, Iowa
Chapter 19	Camellia Gardens, Caringbah, Australia
Chapter 20	Front Porch, Springhill Farm, Iowa
Chapter 21	The inside of a hollowed out tree branch, Springhill Farm, Iowa
Chapter 22	The Esplanade wall, Cronulla Beach, Australia
Chapter 23	Springhill Farm, Iowa
Chapter 24	Back roads of Bertram, Iowa
Chapter 25	The Esplanade wall, Cronulla Beach, Australia
Chapter 26	The cow field beneath the willows, Springhill Farm, Iowa

All characters in this story are true depictions of real people. Most names are adjusted for personal privacy, but kept true to the bearer for the understanding and protection of strangers.

An Original uStory from

Story in the Wings, by Gregga J. Johnn

All Rights reserved by Gregga J. Johnn December 2013

Made in the USA
Charleston, SC
10 July 2015